THREE

TIMES

THE

TROUBLE

C Phillips & D Roach

ISBN-13: 978-1481191807

ISBN-10: 1481191802

Three Times the Trouble - First published 2012

Copyright © 2012 by C Phillips and D Roach

Disclaimer and Medical disclaimer

The descriptions of the symptoms of hypothyroidism experienced by some of the fictional characters within this book were inspired by some of the symptoms that the identical twin authors suffered due to hypothyroidism. The descriptions of the alterations to the treatment for hypothyroidism of some of the fictional characters within this book were inspired by some of the alterations to the treatment for hypothyroidism of the identical twin authors. The specific difficulties experienced by the authors of this book due to the lack of correlation between their symptoms of hypothyroidism and their serum thyroid stimulating hormone levels inspired the descriptions of similar difficulties experienced by some of the fictional characters in this book. However, any such mention of thyroid function tests such as the thyroid stimulating hormone test within this fictional book should not be taken as a criticism of such tests in general. Although the various thyroid hormone treatments prescribed for the authors of this book inspired the descriptions of the various thyroid hormone treatments prescribed for some of the fictional characters in this book, any such mention of thyroid hormone treatments should not be taken as either a criticism or an advertisement for any particular thyroid hormone treatment in general. The description of a fictional support group was inspired by the support provided to the authors of this book from a range of individuals and groups. However, the personalities of the characters within this novel, their dialogues, their actions and their circumstances do not resemble the personalities of the authors and the people within their lives, their dialogues, their actions and their circumstances respectively. Similarities to real people or events are purely coincidental. The authors do not accept responsibility for any omission or error, or for any injury, damage, loss, or financial consequences arising from the use of resources mentioned within this book. In this book, the authors have provided information about some of the fictional characters' experiences of hypothyroidism during childhood and adulthood in order to raise awareness about hypothyroidism. The information contained within this book should not be used to diagnose disease or prescribe medicine and the authors and anyone involved in the production of this book assume no responsibility for such action. Anyone requiring diagnosis, monitoring or treatment should always consult a qualified medical doctor on an individual basis. This is *not* a medical book.

About the authors

The authors of this book C Phillips and D Roach are identical twin sisters from Wales. They both have a Bachelor of Science degree with honours and a Master of Science degree. Their first book entitled 'Hypothyroidism in Childhood and Adulthood *A personal perspective and scientific standpoint*' was published by Nottingham University Press in 2006 and was factual. In their first book, they describe their recovery from hypothyroidism in childhood and their recovery from under-treated hypothyroidism in adulthood.

'Three Times the Trouble' is their second book and this time, they have produced a work of romantic fiction. However, their novel highlights the impact of hypothyroidism by showing its effect upon the lives of some of the fictional characters within the story.

Please see www.thyroidbooks.co.uk where more information about C Phillips and D Roach can be found.

Acknowledgements

We would like to acknowledge the achievements of the individuals who worked hard during their lifetime to improve the way in which hypothyroidism is diagnosed, monitored and treated.

We wish to thank all of the individuals who continue to work tirelessly to improve the plight of hypothyroid patients throughout the world.

In addition, we would like to express our gratitude to the medical professionals who enabled us to recover from hypothyroidism during childhood and to recover from under-treated hypothyroidism during adulthood.

Additional thanks go to the individual whose comment inspired us to begin writing this novel. We would also like to thank our family and friends for providing us with encouragement, J Cameron for her help with the editing and D Phillips for his invaluable knowledge of IT. We are also grateful for the marketing advice that we have received.

Chapter 1

It was 1971 when Meredith and her husband Dylan found out that Meredith was expecting. They couldn't hide their delight. The pregnancy progressed well. However, Meredith was taken aback when she was informed by the staff at the local hospital that she was going to be having triplets.

'I'm having triplets!' Meredith exclaimed.

Her brown eyes widened as she glanced at Dylan. It was wonderful news but it was a massive shock.

The triplets came into the world earlier than expected. On the day of their birth, Dylan bought a bouquet of red roses for Meredith. As the triplets were premature, they had to be kept in incubators and remained in the hospital for a short period before being allowed home. Their parents were filled with joy and hope as they brought the triplets home for the very first time.

After much thought, their parents decided to name the three little baby girls Serena, Anwen and Nia. Serena was ten minutes older than Anwen but Nia was ten minutes younger than Anwen. Meredith and Dylan were thrown into the challenge of looking after not just one but three babies.

It didn't seem long before the triplets' first birthday had arrived. Subsequently, they turned two then their third birthday came and went, then their fourth.

They had inherited their parents' brown eyes and their father's dark brown hair. Their mother would tie their hair in ponytails with coloured ribbons and would tie Nia's hair with a blue ribbon, Anwen's hair with a pink ribbon and Serena's hair with a red ribbon. The triplets were growing rapidly and always seemed to be smiling or laughing. Their mother provided structure to their lives, routine and a sense of calm.

In contrast, their father possessed a sense of adventure. He would suggest a change of arrangement without any notice.

One day, when the triplets were four years of age, their mother was preparing lunch. The chicken and potatoes had roasted. The smell of roast chicken pervaded the kitchen. However, outside in the midst of an azure sky, the sun was dazzling. A warm breeze caressed the triplets as they played in the garden wearing identical yellow gingham dresses. Their father owned a restaurant and he was sitting on the garden bench working on new menu plans whilst watching the triplets play. Next, their mother opened the kitchen window.

'Lunch will be ready in a few minutes,' she said.

Their father gathered the triplets together like baby chicks and ushered them into the house. However, when they got back into the house, he negotiated a change of plan.

'Today is glorious, the sun is shining and there's a lovely warm breeze, what is the weather compelling us to do?' he asked.

'It's compelling me to do some washing and put it out on the line, it's a perfect drying day!' stated their mother. 'Wouldn't you agree?'

'No, the weather is compelling us to go for a picnic!' exclaimed their father.

'But, I've prepared the lunch, how do I turn that into a picnic?' asked their mother.

'Picnic!' echoed the triplets in triplicate.

The idea of a picnic sounded wonderful. Their mother negotiated a compromise; they would all have lunch, then go to the beach and have a mini picnic, consisting of sandwiches and fruit. Their father persuaded the triplets' grandmother to join them at short notice.

A little while later, they were all at the beach. At the seashore, their parents held the triplets' hands as everyone paddled at the water's edge. The triplets' feet made shallow imprints in the damp sand. The cold seawater lapped around their ankles.

As each wave rushed towards them, they held onto the grown ups' hands tightly and squealed in delight as they attempted to jump over each wave.

Afterwards, their mother attempted to wipe the sand from their feet and fastened the buckles on their sandals then the triplets giggled as they chased one another in circles on the warm, dry sand further away from the water's edge.

The sand kept being kicked into their sandals so that their feet pressed against uneven bumps of sand and their sandals required regular unbuckling, shaking and re-buckling. Then they sat under a big parasol erected by their grandmother and made sandcastles. Their visit to the beach was followed by a visit to the nearby ice cream parlour.

When they arrived home, their mother persuaded them to take turns to stand in the bath so that she could rinse the sand from their feet and from in between their toes.

Then, the triplets snuggled onto the settee next to their father who informed them that the settee was magic and could fly. He told them to sit tight as he described the imaginary places over which the settee was flying.

The triplets stared at the red and brown patterned carpet in the living room and were enthralled as they conjured up images of the make-believe destinations.

Their mother came into the room, flopped onto a nearby armchair and fanned herself with a magazine as she watched the triplets peeping over the edge of the settee in delight. She marvelled at their seemingly endless supply of energy.

Before long, the triplets started school. Their presence caused a mixture of confusion and delight amongst the other children in their class.

Time soon passed and the fifth birthday of the identical triplets arrived. Nia, Anwen and Serena were excited that it was their birthday. Their mother made sure that the triplets had plenty to eat for their breakfast before they opened their presents. After breakfast, their parents handed them their birthday presents wrapped in coloured paper: blue paper for Nia's present; pink paper for Anwen's present; and red paper for Serena's gift. Nia smiled when she opened her present to see a rag doll with blue hair, Anwen opened the parcel wrapped in pink paper to see a rag doll with pink hair and Serena ripped open the red wrapping paper to reveal a rag doll with red hair. The triplets showed their appreciation by carrying the dolls with them everywhere throughout the day.

Later that day, their parents had invited some family including the triplets' cousin Carys and some of the neighbours to their house for a birthday party.

The triplets stood in a row looking out of the dining room window in anticipation because they knew that their grandmother would be arriving first and they jumped up and down with excitement when they saw her opening their gate and strolling up their garden path.

'Nanna!' they shouted as their grandmother came into the house and they ran to give her a hug.

Their grandmother was carrying an interestingly large box, which was tied with a yellow ribbon. She had come early to help their parents to prepare a birthday buffet. Meredith was grateful for her mother-in-law's help.

Meredith was pleased that her mother-in-law only lived in the next street so was able to visit as often as possible.

'Isn't it amazing just how fast they're growing!' said their grandmother as she watched the triplets running around the dining room table and giggling.

Plates of egg and cress sandwiches cut into little triangles, cheese and pineapple on sticks and fairy cakes were placed on the dining room table.

Soon all the guests had arrived and multi-coloured birthday cards were opened and placed along the windowsill of the dining room. The triplets opened more gifts including quite a few teddy bears.

'Aren't you lucky?' muttered Mr Williams their next-door neighbour as the triplets opened their presents. 'You're spoilt rotten getting such lovely presents.'

After opening their presents, the triplets had insisted on changing into their new ballet dresses and ballet shoes, which were pale pink and had been given to them by their aunt.

The triplets had their dark brown hair tied back with pink ribbons. They adored the costumes and looked identical in them. Everyone was fascinated by how alike the triplets looked when they were in identical outfits.

Their older cousin Carys was twelve years of age, she was an only child and loved her three little cousins and she let Nia, Anwen and Serena take turns to sit on her lap.

After everyone had eaten the buffet, the triplets' parents carried an iced birthday cake into the dining room. On top of the cake, there were five small candles and three ballerina ornaments made of plastic.

Then, when it came to the time to blow out the candles and make a wish, Anwen, Nia and Serena blew out the candles at the same time.

Their father took a photograph of the triplets. What were they wishing for at just five years of age? The smell of vanilla and burnt candles permeated the dining room.

Serena was admonished for trying to poke her finger into the soft buttercream on the side of the birthday cake. Then their father made sure that the triplets were standing a safe distance away before he took a large knife and began to slice up the birthday cake. Their grandmother put the kettle on and started making cups of tea for the adult guests. Their mother placed individual slices of sweetly fragranced, freshly made birthday cake onto separate paper plates with white serviettes, which were handed to the guests. Everyone enjoyed the birthday cake.

When nearly all the guests had left, the triplets' grandmother busied herself with the washing of the dishes and Meredith put the dishes away. Dylan kept an eye on the triplets whilst they played with their birthday presents in the living room.

The large box that their grandmother had brought had contained a toy china tea set for the triplets to share. That evening, they pretended to have another birthday tea party with their dolls. Serena pretended to pour tea and milk into the tiny cups and served the dolls and teddy bears with cups full of air. The triplets played happily and energetically. Then, their parents told them that it was time to go to bed.

Their house was smaller than their parents would have liked, so the triplets shared a bedroom, which gave them the opportunity to talk or whisper to each other before going to sleep. Their parents had bought the house before they ever knew that they were going to have triplets and knew that at some point in the future, a bigger house would be needed. Their parents read the triplets a story before saying goodnight. When their parents shut the door to the triplets' bedroom, they could hear the sound of the triplets giggling for quite a while until the triplets eventually stopped talking and fell asleep.

However, whilst the triplets were still five years of age, things started to go wrong...

Chapter 2

The triplets were made aware that things weren't right by the reactions of others. One day, five year old Nia overheard her mother and one of her mother's friends talking in the kitchen.

'I'm worried about Nia, she's putting on weight. She is quite chubby compared to her sisters,' their mother said.

'I wouldn't worry about Nia's chubbiness, that's just puppy fat, my daughter had that at the same age, but it disappeared once she got a bit older,' replied their mother's friend reassuringly.

'But the triplets are all eating *the same diet*!' said their mother in a puzzled tone of voice.

'Perhaps Nia's doing less…'

'But I've also noticed that the skin on Nia's scalp is thick and dry. I've started to use a different shampoo for her hair but it doesn't appear to be making any difference, there's no improvement in her scalp,' their mother continued.

'Have a bit of patience, the shampoo will sort the problem soon,' said their mother's friend dismissively.

On one occasion, the triplets came home from school with their mother. On arriving at the front door, their mother fumbled in her handbag and realized that she didn't have her house keys.

'Oh dear!' she sighed. 'We'll have to pop next door to ask Mr Williams if we may use his phone.'

They knocked on his door and Mr Williams answered and peered at them through his silver-rimmed spectacles with a stern expression on his face.

'I'm terribly sorry to bother you,' said their mother.

'What's the problem?' asked Mr Williams.

11

'I'm terribly sorry but I've locked myself out. Please could I use your phone to ask my husband to come home early so that we can get in using his set of keys?'

Mr Williams agreed but didn't look too pleased at being disturbed. They entered his hallway and the triplets were ushered into the parlour, which smelt of tobacco and furniture polish and appeared to be laden with antique furniture. Mr Williams and their mother remained in the hallway so that their mother could use the phone, which was located by the front door.

Through the open door, the triplets could hear their mother speaking on the phone. Mr Williams came into the parlour to ask the triplets if they wanted some tea and biscuits.

'On second thoughts, perhaps that's not a good idea,' said Mr Williams looking at Nia. 'One of you already looks like a little barrel; you've obviously been overindulging on the biscuits!'

Serena glared at him as he went into the kitchen. 'I don't like him being nasty to Nia,' whispered Serena to Anwen.

Serena clenched her fists and proceeded to take off her shoes, clamber onto his settee, and jump up and down on the settee.

'Serena, stop that at once!' exclaimed their mother as she entered the room. 'Come on you three! We'll leave Mr Williams in peace and go and wait for your father in our garden.'

She grabbed Serena's hand and hurriedly thanked Mr Williams. Then, she took the triplets home.

'What on earth possessed you to behave in such a way?' asked their mother. 'I hope that you won't behave in such a terrible way again!'

Serena crossed her arms and looked at her mother defiantly, 'Mr Williams is the *terrible one* and shouldn't say nasty things to Nia!'

However, despite the fact that the three sisters were eating the same diet, Nia was gaining weight and becoming increasingly tired.

Every month, their parents would measure the heights of the triplets against a height chart in the shape of a giraffe pinned to the back of the triplets' bedroom door. They were concerned that as time passed, Serena and Anwen were increasing in height as expected but Nia's growth had slowed.

The triplets knew that their parents were concerned because there would be frequent trips to the general practitioner and long waits in the waiting room after which their mother would thrust the three of them into the consulting room and ask what could be done to help Nia. Baffled, the general practitioners had blamed anaemia for the tiredness and overeating for the weight gain. The general practitioners instructed the triplets' mother to give Nia a calorie controlled diet.

As a result, Nia was subsequently given salads and low calorie lemonade whilst Serena and Anwen were given the same foods as usual.

On a hot day, the low calorie lemonade looked appealing but it was out of bounds for Serena and Anwen. They weren't happy that they were being given different meals from Nia. However, the special diet made no difference to Nia.

On the triplets' sixth birthday, Anwen and Serena could still fit into their ballet dresses but although Nia hadn't grown to the same height as Anwen and Serena, her waistline was broader than their waistlines and to her dismay, her ballet dress no longer fitted.

The triplets' mother took Nia back to the general practitioner on repeated occasions. However, she was told to be patient and to continue to provide Nia with the calorie controlled diet.

Nia had also started to find her schoolwork a struggle. When asked questions in class, she began to find it difficult to provide the correct answers. The class teacher was very impatient with Nia. Anwen and Serena felt powerless to do anything about this.

Furthermore, Nia continued to suffer from exhaustion. Even playing in the playground during the breaks between lessons was too much of an effort for Nia and she would spend breaks sitting on the wall of the playground. Anwen and Serena were worried about Nia because she didn't have the energy to play with them anymore.

Their mother was asked to attend a meeting at the school and because Nia was having trouble with her schoolwork, their mother was informed that Nia was going to be transferred to a different class from Anwen and Serena.

When Serena and Anwen were told this, they were upset, they loved being in the same class and things wouldn't be the same if Nia were in a different class. Serena and Anwen were appalled at the injustice of Nia's impending move to a different class and when their class teacher was admonishing Nia, Serena and Anwen would feel frustrated but they were unable to do anything about the situation.

The three of them continued to attend the same class until the end of the school year but knew that in September, when the new school year started, they would be in separate classes.

The triplets were too young to be self-conscious about the changes in Nia's appearance. However, some of the other girls in their class were quite aware of the fact that Nia had gained weight and that her growth was stunted. As a result, Nia was taunted by some of the other girls in the school playground.

'Why are you so short and fat when your two sisters are so tall and thin?' they asked Nia who then burst into tears.

'Please leave our sister alone!' Anwen and Serena pleaded.

Once Nia was demoted to the lower class, things became even more difficult because some of the other girls would taunt poor Nia mercilessly: 'Why are you fatter and more stupid than your sisters?' they shouted.

Serena and Anwen would stand either side of Nia, put their arms around her, and glare at the bullies defensively.

Their mother wasn't happy when Serena and Anwen told her what some of the other girls had been saying to Nia in school and tried to comfort Nia telling her that she shouldn't take any notice if other children said mean things.

Despite frequent visits to the general practitioner, their parents received no help for Nia. Two years had elapsed since Nia's initial symptoms. In the meantime, the triplets suffered what they felt was the injustice of being in separate classes. Serena and Anwen made up their minds to cause maximum disruption to the teachers. The triplets wore identical clothes and carried identical bags but because they were in different classes, they had different schoolbooks. Therefore, during break time Serena and Anwen would take it in turns to swap their bag with Nia so that they could tell the teacher that they'd mixed up their bags and needed to walk through the school building to swap bags with Nia. This would give them an excuse to see her during their lessons.

The triplets' parents spent many a night discussing their concerns that Nia was just not developing like her sisters. They were at a loss as to what to do because so far their frequent visits to see the doctor hadn't provided any solutions to the problem.

Chapter 3

'I've made up my mind, I'm taking Nia to the doctor's again,' said their mother. 'And I'm not willing to leave until Nia is given an appointment with a paediatrician as a matter of urgency.'

The triplets' mother had planned to take Nia to the doctor's on the following afternoon. However, prior to that, the triplets had to go to their dentist for a routine check-up. After their dental appointment, the dentist called their mother Meredith to one side and asked her if they were identical triplets.

'Yes, they are!' exclaimed their mother.

'Well,' said the dentist rather apologetically, 'Nia's dental development is two years behind Serena and Anwen's dental development.'

Their mother told the general practitioner about this when she took Nia for an appointment that afternoon. The general practitioner arranged for Nia to see a paediatrician. Nia's condition had mystified the general practitioners but on seeing Nia, the paediatrician was certain that she knew what was wrong.

'I'll need to carry out some tests to check but I'm sure that Nia's *severe* symptoms are due to hypothyroidism!' said the paediatrician.

'I'm so relieved that someone seems to know what's wrong at long last!' muttered their mother.

Various tests were carried out. Nia was given blood tests, her chest was covered in a special cream and sensors attached to wires were put on her chest, and she was given an X-ray. She was told that she did indeed have hypothyroidism and she would be provided with prescriptions of thyroxine, a synthetic thyroid hormone to treat this condition. The thyroxine tablets would need to be taken every day for the rest of her life. The correct dose was carefully calculated by her paediatrician.

Just over two years had elapsed between the point at which Nia first started to develop symptoms of hypothyroidism and the point at which she was diagnosed by the paediatrician. By then, Nia was just over seven years of age.

Nia began taking daily tablets of the mysterious substance called thyroxine. To Serena and Anwen, the tablets seemed like magic tablets because once Nia began taking them, she gradually improved. Her energy levels increased and she began to have the energy to play games with her two sisters again. She became more like her previous lively self. Her growth restarted and she became slimmer. With each passing month, she became closer in height and size to Serena and Anwen. Her complexion improved and she lost the yellow pallor that she had acquired.

When the triplets were eight, their father decided that it would be a good idea if they moved house.

'I like the idea of moving house and making a fresh start. I think it will be good for the triplets to go to a different school away from the bullies who taunted Nia,' he said.

'I quite agree,' said their mother. 'We can put this difficult time behind us.'

They moved to an old house in another village in South Wales. The house had thick stone walls and slate on the roof. Inside the house, there was a mix of modern and old-fashioned items. Through the windows at the front of the house, it was possible to admire the view of a river and the surrounding mountains. The house was bigger than their previous house and the triplets were able to have a room each. Their mother was a piano teacher and the house was often filled with the sound of their mother playing the piano.

17

Their mother taught each of the triplets to play the piano. However, only Serena pursued this interest. When their mother wasn't playing the piano, she would be playing records on the record player. Her tastes were eclectic and ranged from classical to popular music.

In their new school, Nia had been placed in the same class as Anwen and Serena. The triplets would be able to spend Saint David's day (which takes place on the first of March) together. The triplets looked forward to participating in the annual Saint David's day celebrations and when the day arrived, they wore traditional Welsh costumes, which had been sewn for them by their grandmother. On top of their white cotton underdress, they each wore a red and black checked skirt, which was covered with a white and black checked apron. They also wore a type of jacket in a black and red striped material. They each wore a woven shawl made of Welsh wool. Their long hair was partially hidden by a tall black hat tied below their chin with a long white satin ribbon. A yellow daffodil was fastened to each shawl. Their father took a few photographs of the triplets and whilst they were in school, their mother took the photographic film to be developed. On arrival at school, nearly all the other girls were adorned in Welsh costumes of a similar description, though some had red skirts with a black stripe along the bottom and white aprons trimmed with lace and some wore paisley shawls. Most of the girls had daffodils pinned to their shawls and nearly all of the boys had leaks pinned to their lapels.

The triplets were delighted to wear their Welsh costumes. When their grandmother had created their costumes, she had carefully sewn tucks and folds into the petticoats and skirts so that the folds could be adjusted on an annual basis so that their costumes became wider and longer as they grew taller.

Before they left their house, their mother had given each of the triplets a box wrapped in white paper tied with a red ribbon. They tore away the ribbons and paper and removed the lids to reveal a little doll wearing a miniature Welsh costume in each box. They insisted upon taking the dolls with them to school. By the mid-morning break, Nia had a sinking feeling in her stomach when she realized that she had mislaid her doll.

She looked everywhere that she could think of for the doll: the cloakroom with its multi-coloured coat hooks, the classroom, the playground, the school hall. She even asked some of the other children in the school hall if they had seen her doll. The other children shook their heads. They hadn't seen it. However, one boy began to search the school for the missing doll.

Finally, Nia gave up looking for the doll and tears welled in her eyes as she sat on the wall of the playground, she sighed and stared at her black shoes. It was at this point that the boy with auburn hair, green eyes and a freckled face who'd been searching for the doll came up to her and handed her the doll and told her that he'd found it on the staircase. Nia thanked him and introduced herself. He told her that his name was Owen. That was the day that Nia first talked to Owen.

As part of the Saint David's day celebrations, the young children spent the remainder of the morning taking part in their school concert in the school hall, which had been adorned with their crayoned drawings of the Welsh flag. During the celebrations, everyone sang Welsh songs and recited Welsh poetry.

Their parents were jubilant when they collected the photographs of their eight year old triplets in their Welsh costumes because in the photographs the triplets looked identical once again. However, more trouble was on its way…

Chapter 4

Whilst the triplets were still eight years of age, Anwen found that when walking short distances or climbing stairs, she would feel breathless. She didn't ask Serena or Nia if they were feeling breathless too. She assumed that they must be. She assumed that all eight year olds felt the same way and became out of breath easily. She said nothing to her parents. However, when walking with Serena and Nia, Anwen began to notice that they would always be a few metres ahead of her and somehow, no matter how hard she tried, she just couldn't keep up with them.

Anwen found all physical activity tiring. This time it was her turn to sit on the school wall during playtime whilst Nia and Serena ran around the playground. However, she didn't complain to anyone and several months passed.

One Saturday, the triplets' father decided that it would be a good idea if they took the triplets for a picnic. As they walked over the grassy fields, Nia and Serena skipped and ran a few metres ahead. Anwen, on the other hand, found herself a few metres behind her parents. No matter how much she tried, she couldn't manage to keep pace with them. Even if they stopped and waited for her to catch up, a few moments later, she would be behind them again.

Their parents laid out a picnic and their mother passed the triplets food to eat. After eating their food, Serena and Nia chased each other around the field but Anwen sat placidly on the picnic blanket, she didn't have the energy to run.

'I'm worried that Anwen's got hypothyroidism like Nia,' whispered their mother to their father.

'Perhaps there's another explanation.'

'What other explanation could there be?'

'Perhaps, she's about to go down with a chest infection or something,' suggested their father.

'Well, let's keep a close eye on her over the next couple of months,' said their mother anxiously.

However, over the next couple of months, Anwen began to put on weight and her cheeks became fuller. Some of the other girls in school started to tease Anwen and she began to feel very self-conscious about her weight and her appearance. She also felt more tired than usual.

Their parents persuaded the general practitioner to provide Anwen with an appointment to see the paediatrician and Anwen was put on a waiting list. By their ninth birthday, Nia, Serena and Anwen no longer looked like identical triplets; Nia and Serena looked like identical twins and Anwen looked like their sister. Again, when the paediatrician saw Anwen, she knew straight away that Anwen was also hypothyroid. After various tests, Anwen was prescribed thyroxine too to treat her hypothyroidism and gradually felt less out of breath, less tired and lost her surplus weight.

By their tenth birthday, they looked more like identical triplets again. However, whilst they were ten years of age, Serena started to suffer from the symptoms of hypothyroidism.

The night before their eleventh birthday, Anwen and Nia found Serena lying on her bed with tears trickling down the sides of her face.

'What's wrong?' asked Anwen anxiously.

'It's our eleventh birthday tomorrow and I wanted to tidy my books and games away before our birthday.'

'We can help you,' said Anwen.

'I know what I want to do in my mind but I haven't got the energy to do it,' explained Serena. 'Trying to get things done also makes me feel out of puff.'

Anwen and Nia glanced at one another. They knew what it felt like to have low energy.

'Tell us what to do and we'll do it,' said Anwen firmly.

'Well, I wanted to put all of my books onto the bookshelf but I am too tired after being at school all day,' stated Serena.

'I'll do that,' said Anwen.

'And I wanted to put all my games into the boxes in the corner of the room.'

'I can do that,' responded Nia.

'Thanks both!' said Serena before smiling weakly.

'Perhaps you've got hypothyroidism too,' suggested Anwen.

'Perhaps I have,' said Serena. 'Unlike you two, I've gradually become chubbier and some of the girls in school have been making fun of me as a result.'

Fortunately, Serena was referred to their paediatrician then diagnosed with hypothyroidism and treated with thyroxine more promptly than either Nia or Anwen had been. All three were being prescribed the same dose of thyroxine.

'At least, we are true triplets again,' said Serena to her sisters when she took her thyroxine treatment for the first time.

Serena gradually improved once taking thyroxine: she gained energy, was no longer breathless when walking and gradually lost her surplus weight.

All three of them would require lifelong treatment for their hypothyroidism.

Chapter 5

The triplets were looking like identical triplets once again. However, their parents had been concerned that whilst they had been in their previous schools, the triplets had all experienced bullying and so it was hoped that now that they were in their secondary school this would not happen.

The triplets' experience did make their parents question how difficult it might be for a child to be diagnosed with hypothyroidism if they were not one of triplets and there was no one with whom their appearance could be directly compared.

The triplets, however, experienced a quiet sense of satisfaction that their hypothyroidism was being treated thus enabling them to have regained their parallel growth and development. In their new school, the triplets were not obliged to tell anyone about their hypothyroidism and although they had developed quite different personalities, the other pupils got confused about which one of the triplets was which.

'What's it like to be an identical triplet?' asked one pupil.

'Are you telepathic?' asked another.

'If one of you is in pain, do the other two of you feel the pain?' asked a third.

They each loved being one of triplets, even though there would be occasional clashes between Nia who tended to be more of an introvert and Serena who tended to be more of an extrovert. Anwen was the diplomat and always managed to resolve any arguments between her two sisters.

What could be better than being born with two ready-made best friends? Perhaps being born a twin would be less fun and being born one of quadruplets would be even more fun but they couldn't imagine what it was like to be an only child.

Although they were alike in looks, they had unique personalities. However, their parents wished to encourage them to develop their own unique identities further so that they could mix better with others with similar interests to their own. From their thirteenth birthday onwards, therefore, their parents used birthdays as an opportunity to give them different presents from one another.

As requested by the triplets, Nia would receive presents with a scientific theme such as a microscope, science books or a chemistry set. Anwen would be given recipe books and Serena was always given something to do with the performing arts such as a musical instrument. In addition, their parents paid for Serena to have singing lessons and drama lessons. Thus, the triplets were encouraged to pursue their individual interests.

Nia maintained that when she grew up, she was going to be a scientist. Anwen loved spending time with her father at his restaurant and she enjoyed helping her grandmother to make a range of dishes. Therefore, she decided that she was going to be a chef. Serena, on the other hand, loved music and was quite confident that she would become some sort of musician or singer.

The summers weren't complete until their friend Owen had cycled to the house where the triplets lived. The four of them played in the fields surrounding the house throughout the warm days of the holidays.

They would climb trees but Owen would be more daring and he would climb higher, then Nia would beg him to climb back down.

They would get hot and dusty and would pour themselves ice-cold glasses of cream soda or lemonade to which they would add some ice cream. The ice cream would cause the lemonade to fizz up to the top of each glass.

The triplets also reaped the benefits of their father's fondness for gardening as a hobby. They were frequently provided with fresh produce from his greenhouse including succulent tomatoes that had been ripened and warmed by the sun.

In the autumn, they would collect baskets of blackberries and help their mother make plenty of blackberry pies to be eaten with warm custard.

However, when Nia, Anwen and Serena were fourteen years of age, the family moved to a house that was much larger than average. The main front door led into a hallway. A staircase led from the hallway up into the second and third floors of the house. Anwen usually looked on the positive side of life and decided that it was an excellent way to increase their exercise levels, as it was necessary to climb two flights of stairs instead of one. Nia was disappointed that they wouldn't be having their usual visits from Owen, as he was no longer in cycling distance.

The triplets progressed well with their schoolwork. They soon made new friends who then came to visit them at their new house. Nia missed Owen's visits but threw herself into her studies and had excellent results. Serena enjoyed living in a more spacious house because she could play the piano without worrying about disturbing the rest of her family. The triplets had excellent exam results and continued at the same school to do their 'A' levels. They waited in suspense for the results of their 'A' levels to find out if they'd achieved sufficiently good marks to enable them to get into university.

Chapter 6

'Fantastic!' said Anwen on seeing her 'A' level results.

She would be able to study food science at university. Then, she quickly looked at her sisters to see the expression on their faces to check that they had passed their exams too. Anwen wouldn't have felt happy if she had done well and her sisters hadn't.

'Wow! I can't believe it, I'll be able to go to university to study music,' said Serena as she looked at her results and found that she'd passed too.

'Well done! I've passed too! I'll be going to university to study biochemistry! Can you believe it?' asked Nia.

'Congratulations Nia! Congratulations Serena!' said Anwen before smiling and hugging her sisters.

It felt like a new chapter had opened in their lives. Nia who had struggled with schoolwork when she'd been younger was particularly relieved to have done just as well as her sisters. Their parents made a fuss to show how proud they were of the triplets and they all had a meal at their father's restaurant.

The triplets were offered and accepted places at the same university. However, they were going to be studying different subjects.

The day that the triplets were due to leave for university arrived. Nia and her sisters finished packing ready to go.

Their grandmother promised them that at the start of each new term at university, she would make them a big tin of Welsh cakes to take back with them. She was mindful of the fact that they would miss visiting her and having a chat and some of her Welsh cakes while they were at university but at least Nia, Anwen and Serena would have some of her Welsh cakes to share with their friends.

Some people made plain Welsh cakes or added lemon flavouring but their grandmother always added mixed spice to her Welsh cakes.

It had been difficult to decide what to take and what to leave behind but Nia had made a list of all that they needed to pack. All Serena had to do was to sit on one of her suitcases to compress the mound of clothes inside so that she could succeed in shutting the case.

The rest of their bags and cases were piled up in the hallway of their house in South Wales. Nia was looking forward to reading all the academic books that she had bought in advance of her course.

Nia walked around the house checking that she hadn't forgotten anything. She looked inside the parlour, which was crowded with photos. There were many photos of the triplets when they were younger.

As usual, Anwen was dressed smartly. She wore a pale pink blouse and matching pink skirt. Anwen tiptoed into the living room and asked her mother if she would mind if she took one of the many magazines on the coffee table to look at during her journey to her university lodgings. Anwen looked in the library, the conservatory, the kitchen and her bedroom to check that she hadn't forgotten to pack anything.

The triplets' mother was looking serene and was being her usual encouraging and enthusiastic self. She wore her long blonde hair knotted on the top of her head in a bun. She looked lovely in her lilac dress and purple cardigan. However, the triplets had the feeling that their mother was putting on a brave face.

The triplets knew that they would miss their daily chats with their mother over a cup of tea but they mustered as much enthusiasm as they could for the new chapter that lay ahead in their lives. They promised that they would phone home and send letters at regular intervals.

Their father was very organized and it was not long before the triplets' entire luggage had been loaded into the boot of his car. He tapped his watch as he urged the triplets to put on their coats and shoes. There was a definite chill in the air as the triplets walked from the house to the car and they could see their breath due to the coldness of the air.

After a few hours of travel, the triplets arrived at the university in England where they planned to spend the next three years of their lives. They were delighted that they would all be studying at the same university as each other. Their parents said goodbye to them before returning home.

Now at eighteen years of age, the triplets had left home for the first time, they couldn't help feeling a pang of anxiety, but they also felt a surge of excitement. Their hostel rooms were basic and each room contained a bed, a desk, a chair, a wardrobe and a sink. The rooms seemed so small compared to their bedrooms at their parents' house. Serena unpacked some of her things and found places for them in her hostel room, which would be her home for the forthcoming year. She unpacked her kettle and filled it with water ready to make a mug of tea to drink while she was unpacking the rest of her things. Serena glanced around her room and half considered the possibility of putting up mirrors on the walls of the room to make it seem bigger. However, she made it look increasingly homely as she unpacked her ornaments.

A moment later, she was startled to hear a knock on her door. She answered the door to see a young man with blue eyes and light brown hair. He was smiling.

'Hi, my name's Stuart, I'm in the room next to yours. How is the unpacking going?'

'Hi, I'm Serena. I'm making good progress with the unpacking, thanks. In fact, I was just about to make a cup of tea, would you like one?'

'Yes please!' replied Stuart. 'Have you had to travel far to get here?'

'Well, I'm from South Wales, so it took a few hours to get here,' responded Serena.

Stuart was studying music too. He bombarded Serena with questions about which modules she was taking as they sat on Serena's bed drinking a cup of tea and eating a couple of Welsh cakes from her grandmother's tin.

'What do you think of the Welsh cakes?' asked Serena.

'They're lovely.'

'I'm glad that you like them. My grandmother made them.'

'My grandmother made me a cake too. I'll have to share some with you tomorrow.'

Serena chatted animatedly and Stuart listened.

'Would you like to join me at the party in the refectory tonight organized to welcome new students?' enquired Stuart.

'Yes, that would be brilliant,' responded Serena immediately.

'I think that we are going to have great fun together at this university,' Stuart said in a triumphant manner. 'Well I may be wrong, we may be in for a dreadful time but I think it's better to be optimistic than realistic but miserable.'

Serena was looking forward to all the social events that were advertised on posters around the campus.

Later that evening, as Stuart walked to the party, he thought that he could see Serena walking towards him.

'Hi, I'm on my way to the party now,' said Stuart. 'Are you coming?'

'No thank you, I'm on my way to the library at the moment,' responded Nia politely but with a slightly puzzled expression on her face.

Chapter 7

When Stuart entered the party, he saw Serena standing by the bar and looked confused: 'You just said you were going to the library, how come you're here and wearing something different?'

Serena laughed, 'I guess I forgot to say that I'm one of identical triplets. My two sisters are at university with me as well, so if you saw someone who looks like me going to the library, that was probably Nia.'

The first week was a whirl of activity. Nia found herself spending the days attending lectures or doing work in the laboratory. However, in the evenings, she spent some time in the library. When she attended parties, she arrived as late in the evening as possible.

After the first week, the parties were less frequent and the work intensified but Nia worked hard to meet all the demands placed upon her at university. The triplets had been reminded by their father that an education at university was a great opportunity that shouldn't be wasted. Nia didn't want to disappoint herself by not trying her best as she faced a range of challenges. Thus, she tended to spend the evenings working in the library.

Serena, on the other hand, tried to avoid spending too long in the library and preferred to take the books back to her room so that she could listen to music. In addition, she seemed to know when any parties were occurring.

Anwen tried to balance her time carefully between her academic work and the social activities that Serena let her know about. Anwen tried to please both Nia and Serena and worried about whether she would succeed in balancing the competing demands that they made.

The triplets took the opportunity to make friends with students not just from the United Kingdom but also from all over the world.

Whilst at university, Nia, Anwen and Serena developed their individual dress codes. Nia tended to wear navy blue or black T-shirts and jeans and nearly always wore her hair in a ponytail. Anwen preferred white, cream and pale pink garments and often wore flowing dresses with a matching hair band. However, Serena preferred fitted dresses and high-heeled shoes. The dresses that she wore were normally in vibrant colours such as red, cerise, turquoise, emerald green or purple. Their ideas about make-up also differed; Nia wore a clear lip-gloss; Anwen usually wore a pale pink lipstick whilst Serena favoured a bright red lipstick. Nia would wear perfume if someone had happened to buy her some on a previous birthday. Anwen's presence was usually accompanied by the subtle fragrance of lavender or rose. However, Serena's entrance was always heralded by the aroma of an expensive French perfume.

However, despite these superficial differences, in lots of ways they remained similar. They had the same taste in foods and they enjoyed going out to a variety of restaurants together.

During their first term at university, the weeks were extremely busy but Nia, Anwen and Serena would meet up on a Saturday and have a break from work. They would catch a bus to the town centre and buy provisions then catch up with some letter writing.

On one particular Saturday morning, Stuart joined them. It was a typical autumn day and the falling leaves from the trees looked beautiful. The triplets and Stuart entered a café, which was filled with the aroma of freshly brewed coffee. They sat at a corner table and perused the menu.

'I'm going to have the vegetable soup and a bread roll,' said Serena.

'Me too,' said Nia and Anwen simultaneously.

31

'Do you have the same taste in foods?' asked Stuart.

'Most of the time,' replied Anwen.

'Do you have the same taste in men? That would be quite…'

'Of course not!' interrupted Nia and she changed the subject by continuing with, 'It's nice relaxing today but we're going to have to start the revision for the end of term exams soon.'

'Don't talk about revision! I don't want to start thinking about revision yet,' complained Stuart.

'Let's just enjoy today,' said Anwen sweetly.

They ordered their food and a few minutes later, it was brought to their table.

'This is delicious, it's a change from the canteen,' commented Serena.

'I like the food in the canteen actually,' admitted Anwen, 'especially the pancakes with vegetable sauce and the baked potato with tuna and I've discovered another café on campus where they sell quite nice rolls, I'll have to take you all there next week. It's very popular, it was full of students talking and messing about when I went there.'

'Some of the students don't seem bothered about the forthcoming exams. They seem to take everything in their stride,' said Nia.

'I thought we weren't going to talk about the exams,' Stuart reminded them. 'Anyway, just because they say they're not worried, it doesn't *mean* they're not worried. They're probably trying to lull everyone else into a false sense of security so that they can do revision in secret and get ahead!' said Stuart as he glanced at each of the triplets in turn and watched as their eyes widened in panic.

'You've got me *really* worried now!' exclaimed Anwen. 'Perhaps we should all start doing revision in secret now!'

'I think all three of you are panicking,' said Stuart, 'well, judging by the expressions on your faces.'

'Having the day off today will put us in a better frame of mind,' said Anwen. 'By the way, how was your week Nia?'

'As usual, busy with lots of work to do. Some of the lectures were complex, especially physics, and I started cytology and genetics, and microbiology. In the microbiology practical, we had to look at bacteria under the microscope.'

'Let's talk about something different while we're eating,' said Serena.

'What's the deal with your names?' asked Stuart.

'What do you mean?' asked Serena.

'Well why do Nia and Anwen have what I presume to be Welsh names but not you Serena?'

'Actually,' said Serena proudly, 'even though I don't have a Welsh name, the first part of my name *Seren* happens to mean "star" in Welsh.'

'Does it?' asked Stuart looking impressed.

'By the way, there's something I wanted to give you two,' said Serena turning to Nia and Anwen.

'What is it?' asked Nia.

'I received a letter from our cousin Carys today along with a gift for each of us, so I've brought the letter and gifts with me.'

'May I have a look?' asked Anwen as she leaned across to look at the three key rings that Serena had just pulled out of her bag. 'May I have the pink one, please?'

'Yes, of course,' replied Serena.

'I'll have the blue one,' said Nia.

'Thought so,' said Serena. 'And I'll keep the red one!'

'It's so nice to meet up like this,' said Anwen. 'There's no retreat from intense work unless you want to participate in an intense social life.'

'The intense social life suits me!' said Stuart.

'I'm looking forward to returning home Christmas time and actually relaxing, which you can't really do at university,' said Anwen.

'Yes, after a term at university, we'll really be able to enjoy Christmas,' said Serena enthusiastically.

'Well as long as we succeed in getting through our first lot of exams and don't get chucked out...' said Nia.

'You three worry too much!' interjected Stuart.

'Well you started us off by saying that everyone might be revising in secret,' said Nia.

'I was half joking,' replied Stuart.

'Well, I hope we all pass our first lot of university exams!' exclaimed Anwen.

Chapter 8

Christmas arrived and went by far too quickly for the triplets' liking but they were relieved when they received their results and found out that they had all passed all of their first university exams.

They returned to university for their second term. During the second week of term, it snowed and the snow was quite deep. They met up in Serena's room to read their letters from home together.

'I wonder what the weather's been like in South Wales,' said Anwen.

'It's a pity that we live on campus, the snow isn't stopping us from getting to lectures, if we lived off campus we might not be able to get in,' said Serena.

'I have to do some biochemistry next,' said Nia, 'I have a practical to write up and some reading to do.'

'I have quite a lot of work to do too later,' complained Serena, 'I have an assignment that has to be handed in next week.'

'The more we work, the busier our timetable gets,' said Anwen.

'By the way, Stuart and a couple of his friends are going to the cinema on Friday evening and asked if we wanted to go,' said Serena.

'Really!' exclaimed Anwen.

'And on Saturday, they said that we're welcome to go to the pub with them and a few other girls. And on Sunday, a few girls in my hostel have asked if we want to join them for a walk,' continued Serena.

'But we don't have the time to do all of our assignments and take up every single invite,' cautioned Nia.

'But it's still early in the term, so let's make the most of things until our workload gets even heavier,' said Serena.

'We'll have to wrap up warm before going out this week, it's *bitter* cold, the snow's deeper and it's also very windy,' warned Anwen with a concerned expression on her face.

During the next week, the triplets had full timetables but the following Saturday, Stuart asked them if they wanted to go to the nearby town with him. The roads were quite clear but there was a lot of slushy brown snow on the edge of the roads.

They bought groceries and chatted to one another as they walked through the town back to Stuart's car.

'I wish I was managing to get more work done each week,' moaned Serena. 'Piano practice takes up a large percentage of my time.'

'Yes, food chemistry practicals take up most of my time,' said Anwen.

'What sort of things are you doing in food chemistry?' asked Serena.

'Well last week, everyone had an unknown sugar to identify, mine was fructose. We had to do various chemical tests and the sugars had to be boiled with different chemicals in a test tube so that colour changes could be noted.'

'Do you enjoy the food chemistry practicals?' asked Serena.

'Well you have to be careful, I always make sure that I wear safety glasses but I'm always pleased when the practicals go smoothly and the results are of interest,' concluded Anwen.

'Hey, what are you all doing for the rest of the afternoon?' asked Stuart.

'I'm going to write some letters,' said Anwen.

'I think that I'll try to get some work done,' replied Nia.

'I have choir practice later this afternoon,' said Serena.

'Well it seems that you all have plans but if you're free next Saturday, we could all go into the neighbouring city centre, look around the shopping centres and the adjoining streets and get to know our way around. There's a great café there where they serve pancakes,' said Stuart.

'That sounds lovely,' said Serena. 'I went there a few times last term and I was struck by its size, it has a mixture of majestic grand old buildings, modern shops and quaint old fashioned pubs.'

'Have you all bought enough food for the week?' asked Stuart.

'Yes,' replied Anwen.

'Well, we'll drop the groceries back at campus but who'd like to go to the café on campus for a quick coffee?' asked Stuart.

'I'd love to go,' replied Serena. 'It's such a lovely day; the sky's so clear and blue.'

Nia and Anwen declined the offer so Serena agreed to go to the café with Stuart on her own.

'I rarely have the chance to speak to you on your own,' said Stuart. 'You always bring Anwen and Nia.'

'Well, you are friends to all three of us,' said Serena blushing. 'I assumed that we were all invited.'

'Of course, you're all welcome to join me for social arrangements but I was wondering if you'd like to go on a date with me?'

'Yes, well yes actually, I'd love that.'

'Well, would you like to go to a concert with me on Saturday evening in a fortnight's time?'

'That sounds wonderful.'

The next day, Stuart visited Serena for a cup of tea and it was the start of a new phase in their relationship.

After the Easter break, the triplets arrived back at university for the final term of their first year: the summer term. After their parents had left, they unpacked relatively quickly.

All of the cherry blossom trees had flowered over Easter. The gardens looked beautiful and the air was full of birdsong.

Serena gave Stuart a Welsh love spoon carved out of wood. She had bought it for him over the Easter break.

Some of the other girls in the hostel visited the triplets and everyone moaned about how little work they'd done over Easter.

All three of the triplets had exams again at the end of the first year summer term. Towards the end of the term, they were very busy with revision. While they were inside revising, the weather was glorious and the second year students were sitting outside on the lawns.

As the exams got nearer, the triplets felt an increasing sense of panic and were obliged to spend as much time as possible doing revision during the evenings and weekends. They revised until the very last minute before each exam.

When the exams were over, the triplets met up for a cup of coffee.

'I don't know if I wrote a load of irrelevant waffle or if it will get me enough marks to pass,' moaned Serena.

'I know the feeling, we've worn ourselves out revising, we've been going to bed late and getting up early but we've tried our best so we should try not to think about the exams now,' advised Anwen.

'I know, it's been a really difficult time, every morning I was trying to fit in some revision before the first exam of the day,' commented Nia.

'And I wasn't able to spend much time with Stuart,' complained Serena.

'None of our exams were easy but we have done a lot of revision so hopefully we'll pass,' said Nia.

'Remember, no more talk about the exams,' chided Anwen.

'Well at least they are over,' said Nia cheerfully.

'Yes, and to celebrate, we'll go shopping on Saturday,' said Serena.

'We usually go shopping on Saturdays,' said Nia.

'*Not* grocery shopping!' said Serena. 'I'm going to buy some new clothes.'

'Then we could go for lunch somewhere,' added Anwen enthusiastically.

'They certainly keep you working and plunge you in at the deep end with a degree,' said Nia. 'So we deserve a break.'

Chapter 9

Fortunately, the triplets passed their first year exams and were able to return to university for their second year after the summer holidays.

Likewise, they passed their second year exams and after their second summer break, they returned to university for their third and final year.

During their final year, the triplets celebrated their 21st birthday together. They visited a delightful café that sold homemade cakes.

'I'll go and order,' announced Anwen. 'Which cake would you both like? Come on, it is our birthday so we could each choose a different one and then we could cut each one in three and try three different cakes at the same time.'

'Yum, which one do I choose?' pondered Nia. 'I'll have the carrot cake, please.'

'I'll go for the strawberry cheesecake but the cream on top has been piped into such an intricate pattern that it looks too pretty to eat!' said Serena.

'Well, I'm going to order the chocolate cake and I'll also order three cups of coffee,' said Anwen as she peered into the glass covered cabinet.

The triplets sat down and chatted. When the coffee and cakes were served, Nia meticulously divided each of the three cakes into three so that the triplets could share all three cakes between themselves.

'Happy Birthday!' said the triplets simultaneously.

They exchanged gifts and laughed when they opened their gifts: Serena had bought gold earrings for Nia and Anwen; Anwen had bought the same earrings for Serena and Nia; and Nia had bought similar gold earrings for Anwen and Serena.

'What are the odds?' asked Serena.

'It's just that our tastes are similar,' said Nia.

'Can you believe that we are twenty one and we're in the third year of university?' asked Serena.

'The first year students seem so young now!' said Anwen.

'Yes, they use the hostel phones for hours at a time,' said Nia.

'But some things don't change, the lecturers are still piling up the work for us,' scowled Serena.

'I have a full timetable, no free lessons, practicals every day and lots of work,' stated Nia.

'But we did find time to go to a fancy-dress party this week,' commented Serena.

'I didn't stay as long as you,' said Nia.

'Well, she did have Stuart's company so she had an ulterior motive to stay longer,' said Anwen. 'It's good that I didn't stay out as late as Serena or I would have been exhausted during my food chemistry practical the next day. It was interesting but difficult. We analysed different margarines for their fatty acid content. We had to use a variety of techniques including gas liquid chromatography and other methods...'

'Sounds interesting!' interjected Serena sarcastically as she faked a yawn.

'I'm sure it was interesting,' said Nia defensively.

'On another topic, do you think it would be a good idea to arrange a surprise birthday party for Stuart?' asked Anwen. 'We could buy stacks of food and invite his friends to come to Serena's room before Stuart is due to arrive.'

'That's a lovely idea!' exclaimed Serena. 'We could get balloons, a tablecloth and cheese and pineapple on sticks.'

'Stuart will be delighted,' said Anwen.

'Yes, and it will be great to have a break from biochemistry,' commented Nia, 'and from lectures about protein isolation and nucleic acid isolation.'

41

The following week, Serena asked Anwen if she would call to see Stuart's best friend in order to invite him to Stuart's surprise party.

Anwen agreed to run and ask him on condition that she could borrow Serena's coat because the weather had become colder that evening. However, before Anwen had a chance to tell Stuart's best friend that Serena was planning a surprise party for Stuart, he mentioned that Stuart had arranged to see family on his birthday. Anwen didn't think that it was worth mentioning that Serena had been planning to arrange a surprise party for Stuart when he wouldn't be at university for his birthday anyway.

Anwen explained to Serena that because Stuart would be seeing his family on his birthday, Serena would not be able to arrange a surprise party for Stuart after all.

The next day, Serena came across Stuart in the library.

'We can't really talk here but may I come and see you later? There's something I want to talk to you about,' whispered Stuart.

'Okay, of course, see you later,' replied Serena and smiled as she left the library. What did Stuart want to talk to her about? Perhaps he wanted to invite her to meet his family when he saw them on his birthday! She was curious now.

When Stuart knocked on Serena's door, Serena opened her door and rushed towards him. She gave him a hug and was surprised when he pulled away from her.

'There's something I want to speak to you about,' stated Stuart as he entered her room.

'What?' asked Serena.

'I don't know if I want to continue our relationship,' declared Stuart.

'But why? I *thought* we were getting on well,' responded Serena.

'That's what I thought but late last night, I saw you leaving my friend's room and you were both laughing.'

'Well, you should know me well enough to be able to trust me by now!' declared Serena. 'Anyway, there is a perfectly innocent explanation…'

Stuart walked out of the room and closed the door behind him before she had the chance to explain everything.

Stuart's best friend informed Stuart it was Anwen who'd visited but that even if it had been Serena who had visited, Stuart should have trusted them both. Stuart felt a bit foolish and subsequently apologized to his best friend and to Serena. However, although they continued dating, Serena was concerned that Stuart hadn't trusted her.

The triplets didn't have so much time to phone or write home during their final summer term at university as they were so busy completing their work and revising for exams. They tried to fit in time to socialize and go to parties occasionally too and even managed to fit in a visit to the theatre with their friends.

However, Serena and Stuart decided that they were too busy to maintain their relationship and were obliged to end things with one another so that they could concentrate on their revision but promised to remain friends.

After the triplets had finished their third and final year exams, they went home for a few weeks. During their first weekend home, they decided to make the most of being able to do things that they hadn't had time to do for a while such as trying out new recipes together.

'Anwen's got quite a few recipe books, let's follow the instructions in one of her books and make a cake,' suggested Nia.

'It would be more fun to improvise and make up our own recipe for a cake with interesting ingredients. Creativity is important,' persuaded Serena.

'I prefer to follow a recipe and if I make an amendment to the recipe, I make a note of it so that if the cake is a success, it can be recreated,' stated Nia. 'Because you don't keep a record of any changes that you make to a recipe, you never remember how to recreate your dishes. Precision is important.'

'You're both half right and half wrong because cooking requires both precision and creativity,' said Anwen, being her usual diplomatic self.

They loved the aroma of baking that filled the kitchen as the cake was cooking and whilst it cooled on a metal rack.

'We could cut the cake into very thin slices so that we'll be able to have more slices, then we'll feel as if we've had more cake,' said Anwen.

'Okay,' said Serena laughing, 'if you insist!'

'Let's relax for a change and watch a film tonight,' suggested Nia. 'Which film shall we watch?'

'As long as the film ends happily, I don't mind which film we watch,' stated Anwen.

'I've seen you look at the last page of a book to check that you like the ending before you read it but you shouldn't worry about that because any story could be considered happy or sad purely by changing the point at which the story ends,' concluded Serena.

'I'm not going to sit watching a sad film,' declared Anwen firmly.

'My main concern would be to find a film with a dramatic plot, *passionate* characters and a surprising ending,' said Serena.

Nia was pensive and said to her sisters, 'Here we are, fussing about what to do together tonight, I wonder what each of us will be doing this time next year?'

'I wonder which one of us will get a job, a house and meet someone special first,' said Serena and grinned at Anwen and Nia.

'I just hope that we all pass our final exams and we all find a career that we love and that we all meet someone wonderful!' said Anwen.

Chapter 10

Fortunately, the triplets all passed their final exams. When they graduated, they booked tickets at the same graduation ceremony and booked guest tickets so that their mother, father and grandmother could attend. They glanced at one another in delight as they strode across campus in their caps and gowns.

'We did it!' exclaimed Serena. 'Those years studying, those late nights and all those ghastly exams were worthwhile!'

'Yes, it was all worth it,' stated Anwen. 'Although there were times when I felt like giving up.'

'Yes, I know, it was quite gruelling at times!' agreed Nia.

Next, they waited patiently in the queue for the photographer and a series of photographs were taken. The ceremony itself was a surreal event. The academic staff stood resplendent in an array of academic gowns of various vibrant colours and organ music filled the hall. They waved to their mother, father and grandmother who were seated together at the back of the hall. Once they'd traversed the stage to be presented with their certificates, they relaxed and paid more attention to the proceedings. The triplets found themselves more moved by the speeches being made by various members of the academic staff than they had expected to be.

After the ceremony, the triplets and their family were ushered into a large room for refreshments. They sipped champagne as they chatted to each other.

For Anwen and Serena, their time at university had ended; Anwen would be working at their father's restaurant, as would Serena until she found herself a job that suited her musical talents. However, Nia had applied to do a Master of Science degree.

Nia had mixed feelings about continuing at university. Being away from home without Anwen and Serena would be a lonelier experience and it would be hard work but she did find science interesting. However, despite her mixed feelings, Nia's application was accepted and she stayed on at university.

During her first week back at university, she rang her parents.

'Hi Dad, how are you? How's Mam?' asked Nia.

'We're all right, how's everything going with you?' enquired her father.

'I'm glad you're okay, I haven't had much chance to phone anyone until now, I've been really busy,' said Nia.

'It's great to hear from you, I think your mother wants to speak to you.'

'How is it all going?' asked her mother.

'I'm starting to get to know other people a little bit now. On Monday, I went to a concert and all the new undergraduate students were milling about. It's quite nice to be a postgraduate and not to have exams. There's a new girl doing the same Master of Science degree as me. Last night, I went out for a meal at her house then we went to a nightclub. It was okay but the music was a bit loud for us,' replied Nia. 'One of the boys in some of my classes is in a band and we saw him there.'

'That's great, I know you've got lots of work but try to balance out the work with other things and with rest if you can so that you don't tire yourself out!'

'Yes, I'll try to keep things balanced. I'd better go now but I'll keep in touch with you with all my news.'

'Okay, you take care! Love you!'

'Love you too! I'll speak to you soon.'

Nia tried to maintain some sort of balance between work and relaxation during her Master of Science degree. However, she loved it whenever Serena or Anwen visited.

One week, Serena came to stop and enjoyed going to the cafés on campus and the social events.

'This reminds me how wonderful it was to be a student!' exclaimed Serena when she met up with Nia during the afternoon.

'You are only remembering the fun times. It's hard work,' stated Nia.

'I guess you're right,' agreed Serena.

'I haven't been having an easy time today, one of the new lecturers must have mistaken you for me because I just had a telling off for spending time in the café this morning when I should have been at one of the seminars. I explained that I had been at the seminar and that he must have seen my identical triplet in the café but he did not seem in the least convinced by my explanation!' complained Nia.

Nia completed her Master of Science degree in 1994. After the summer ball and graduation, she'd be travelling back to Wales to stay with her parents.

Nia had been able to get spare summer ball tickets for Anwen and Serena and they were delighted to stop with her for a few days. The triplets went shopping together to buy something to wear at the final summer ball before Nia left university. Serena was helpful in pointing out the dresses that would suit Nia the best. After trying on a mound of different dresses, Serena chose a red taffeta gown and red heels. Nia chose a long black satin dress and black high-heeled shoes. Anwen chose a pale pink taffeta dress. Feeling satisfied with their purchases, the triplets went for coffee. Shopping for their new outfits had given them all a boost to their mood.

Anwen and Serena were sleeping on camp beds on the floor of Nia's room and got ready in Nia's room on the night of the party. After Serena had put on her make-up, she helped Nia put on her make-up.

Nia didn't usually wear make-up but had decided that because the ball was a special occasion, she would make an exception.

At the venue for the summer ball, Nia found three seats at a table near the stage and the dance floor. It was wonderful to see her fellow students wearing colourful evening dresses, ball gowns or dinner jackets. Silver helium balloons rose above each table and seemed to sway slightly to the beat of the music as if even inanimate objects had been caught up in the joyous atmosphere that pervaded the room. Everyone had received their results and felt entitled to an evening of enjoyment.

Nia glanced at a group of three men in their evening attire standing on the other side of the room across the dance floor in earnest conversation with one another. The man standing in the middle of the group caught Nia's attention, he had striking blue eyes and his blond hair was cut in layers that fell across his forehead and the longest layer brushed the edge of his collar.

Suddenly, Nia became aware that the man in the middle of the group had returned her glance and she felt a twist of excitement in her stomach. Nia glanced back at him and smiled. She hadn't seen him before. If he'd been on campus all year, she would have noticed him. Perhaps he was attending a summer course. Perhaps he was one of the entertainers or musicians.

Her sisters came and joined Nia, resplendent in their elegant dresses. Nia decided not to mention the stranger on the other side of the dance floor. However, throughout the evening, her eyes were drawn to him and she felt aware that from time to time he was returning her glances. On the stage, a woman wearing a white satin dress whose sleek black hair was smoothed into a bun sang a series of ballads. The triplets ordered a cocktail each and chatted whenever the singer paused between songs.

Eventually, the singer announced that there would be a half hour break and that buffet snacks were available at the back of the room.

'Let's go and get something from the buffet!' urged Anwen. 'Quick, let's go before a queue forms!'

'You go, I'm fine, I'll stay here,' said Nia.

Nia was aware that unusually for her, she was wearing deep pink lipstick and a fitted satin dress and she did not relish the idea of her lips and dress becoming dusted with crumbs if she ate a selection of snacks from the buffet. On an ordinary evening, she would have had something to eat but the stranger on the other side of the room had filled her with a strange excitement and she felt compelled to stay within his view. Nia took a sip of her cocktail and stole another glance towards the handsome stranger and she saw that he was crossing the dance floor and walking in her direction.

'How do you do?' he asked.

He held out his right hand as if to shake hands and Nia offered her right hand in return but rather than shaking her hand, he kissed it. At the same time, his leg brushed against her leg and she felt as if his touch had imparted a spark of electricity onto the surface of her hand and leg.

'I'm fine thank you, how do you do?' Nia managed to say.

'I'm okay thank you. My name is Marek, what is your name?'

'My name is Nia, I'm a student here and I come from Wales.'

'Ah, I see! I live in Poland. However, my research team is carrying out a research project in biochemistry in collaboration with a research team at this university. I have been funded to spend the summer here with members of the research team based in the United Kingdom. I'm here for a few weeks.'

'I've just completed a Master of Science degree, so I'll be going home soon and then I'll be returning briefly for the graduation.'

'Congratulations!'

'Thanks! Is it difficult to discuss science in another language to your own?' asked Nia.

'Ah, but the language of science is universal!' replied Marek and grabbed a serviette and drew two molecules plus an arrow and a question mark and passed the serviette and a pen to Nia with the expectation that she would draw the molecule that would result if the two molecules that he had drawn reacted with one another. Fresh from the rigours of studying for her degree, Nia was able to complete the chemical reaction on the serviette. Marek clapped his hands together in appreciation.

Nia threw a glance to the back of the room to see if her sisters were still in the buffet queue and saw them with full plates chatting to each other in the distance.

Marek's enthusiasm for everything around him made Nia's spirit soar so that she felt more excited and enthusiastic about her world and the prospects that it offered.

The singer returned to the stage and the music began again. Then Marek took Nia's hand and beckoned her to dance with him. Marek held her in his arms and swirled her around the dance floor as if they were ballroom dancing. At times, Marek held Nia as close as possible whilst they danced.

Nia felt as if she'd entered a magical world and nothing else seemed to matter. It was one of those perfect nights, she thought to herself. She decided that she owed it to herself to make the most of his company even though she could see that her sisters had returned to the table and were looking in her direction throughout the evening and whispering in one another's ears. They were probably talking about her.

However, at midnight, seemingly without warning, the music stopped and harsh white lighting illuminated the corners of the hall: a stark reminder that it was time for everyone to make their way home.

'Oh, I have to go now, my sisters and I have booked a taxi,' said Nia to Marek. She was filled with disappointment that the ball had ended.

She hadn't needed to take photographs that night because every detail was etched on her memory never to be forgotten. She joined her sisters and they left the hall and walked towards the taxi waiting outside. Nia felt a surge of disappointment.

Chapter 11

As the triplets clambered into the taxi, Nia glanced wistfully towards the party's venue, she felt a surge of excitement when she saw Marek leave the building and run towards the taxi.

'But I shall never see you again!' he cried as he tapped the window of the waiting taxi.

'Don't leave yet!' cried Nia, as she opened the taxi door. 'Does anyone have any paper and a pen?'

Nia's tiny satin evening bag hadn't accommodated her notebook and pen and in her wisdom, she had retained the ability to shut the bag firmly by deciding to omit these items from her bag.

'I haven't got a pen and paper to give you my contact details,' gasped Nia.

'Please meet me tomorrow!' begged Marek.

'Where?'

'We'll meet at the main entrance to the train station near the campus at 6 pm.'

'At the main entrance to the train station at 6 pm,' agreed Nia.

Marek closed the taxi door and the taxi pulled away. Nia looked out of the back window until Marek's figure faded into the distance.

The next day, Nia waited at the entrance to the train station at 6 pm. She saw Marek walking towards the train station. When he saw Nia, he rushed towards her. When they greeted each other, he took her hand and kissed it, which she found charming.

They walked towards a little inn, went inside and ordered two meals. Marek's eyes widened as he talked to Nia. Again, time passed too quickly for Nia and it did not seem long before they had to walk back to the university campus.

It was a beautiful moonlit night and as they walked back, Marek put his arm around Nia and told her the names of some of the stars in the sky.

The next day, they met up with each other for the third time and spent hours together. Marek explained that he would be busy with his research work over the summer.

'Will you meet me before I leave for Poland?' asked Marek.

'Yes, of course!' said Nia

'Thank you!' said Marek.

After a hug, Nia and Marek separated and Nia glanced backwards towards Marek at the same moment that he turned around and waved.

A few weeks later, it was a clear day and Nia sat on a crowded train on her way to meet Marek. Above the hum of the train's engine were the sounds of newspapers rustling and muffled conversations. She glanced out of the window and the scenery reminded her of a delicate decoupage design; the silhouettes of the trees in the foreground overlay the silhouettes of the trees in the background, which stood against the backdrop of a blue sky. The sun glared through the silhouettes of trees. She wished that she could wave a magic wand and be transported instantly to her destination. However, she knew that wasn't possible so she fumbled in her bag and pulled out a paperback. She attempted to focus her attention on the black and white pages but the brightness of the sun made it difficult to concentrate. Nevertheless, she attempted to immerse herself in the lives of the fictional characters portrayed on the pages.

As the train moved forward, the country scene was transformed into a cityscape and the announcement over the intercom prompted her to grab her shoulder bag and shuffle along the aisle behind the queue that had suddenly appeared from the middle of the train carriage to the train door.

She stepped down from the train carriage and made her way to the train station exit where she had arranged to meet Marek on the first occasion.

Commuters bustled past. She glanced at her watch. Five minutes passed by, then ten, then fifteen. She hoped that she wasn't going to be forgotten. She glanced at her watch again.

When she glanced back at the doorway, she saw Marek rushing towards her. He was smiling and clutching a bouquet of red roses. She felt a twist of excitement in her stomach. The next moment, he was by her side.

'Hi, it's wonderful to see you! Where would you like to go?' asked Nia.

'There's a small restaurant nearby, we shall go there,' said Marek.

'That sounds good!' said Nia nodding enthusiastically.

As they sat in the restaurant, Nia found it difficult to stop herself from smiling. They gazed at one another and caught up on one another's news.

'There's something I want to say,' said Marek, 'I'm going back to Poland next week, I've done as much research as I can here and the rest of the research needs to be carried out in Poland but I want to see you again as soon as possible.'

'Yes, I want to see you too,' said Nia.

When they were due to part, Nia looked at Marek and told herself not to start crying. That wouldn't do anyone any good.

Marek gently moved some strands of hair from her face and kissed her lips. Marek looked at her intently and promised her that they would see each other again as soon as possible. However, when the moment came for them to say goodbye, they clung to each other as if they never wanted to let go. Then it was time for Marek to leave. Nia wondered when she would see him again.

Chapter 12

The days turned into weeks and Nia kept herself busy. She wanted to find a job using her qualifications but such jobs were hard to come by and in the meantime, she was working at her father's restaurant with her sisters. However, the highlight of Nia's week was when a letter from Marek appeared on the doormat of their parents' house. Nia would read each letter repeatedly.

One morning, a letter came through in which Marek gave her an ultimatum:

I can't come to Britain at the moment but please my darling, if your feelings for me are real, find a way of coming to visit me in Warsaw or I shall have to assume that your feelings aren't real and I shall have to forget about you forever...

The words haunted Nia; she couldn't bear the thought of being excluded from Marek's life forever. She could visit but that didn't seem good enough. The answer would be to find a job in Poland.

What could she do in Poland? She couldn't speak Polish. She wrote a hurried reply in which she promised to visit Warsaw and see him again soon.

That evening, Nia was working at her father's restaurant. The restaurant had been hired for a party and she made polite conversation with some of the guests. A tall blonde woman in a blue dress struck up a conversation with Nia.

'It's a lovely venue for my farewell party, I already have a degree and I've just completed a qualification that will enable me to teach English to speakers of other languages and I've just got a job in France teaching English,' said the blonde woman.

'Tell me more!' said Nia.

After speaking to the woman and finding out more details, Nia decided that she would do the same qualification then find a job in Warsaw and surprise Marek.

She faced opposition from certain members of her family especially her father but she was determined to continue with her plan.

A few weeks later, she had completed the qualification and had applied for a few jobs in Warsaw. When a letter containing a job offer lodged in the letterbox, she retrieved the letter and tore it open. After reading its contents, she danced around the room.

The next fortnight was hectic, Nia spent the time making lists, buying the additional items that she needed and packing.

'I'll miss you,' said her mother wistfully.

'I'll miss you but it's something that I have to do,' said Nia.

Finally, the day arrived when Nia set out on the long train journey to the airport to get the plane to Warsaw. Although she had two long journeys ahead of her, she believed that all the travelling would seem irrelevant once she was in Marek's arms.

It was late evening when Nia emerged from the airport terminal in Warsaw. An elegant woman with long auburn hair, a black fitted suit and shimmering tights held a card on which Nia's name had been written along with words of welcome.

'I'm Nia, how do you do?'

'Fine, thank you. How are you?'

'Okay, thanks,' replied Nia.

'I'm Agnieszka and I'll be taking you to your accommodation. Tomorrow morning, I'll meet you and show you around. You can relax on Saturday afternoon and Sunday then the job will start on Monday.'

Agnieszka and Nia took a taxi to the outskirts of Warsaw where high-rise buildings dotted the landscape. Nia made a mental note of any unusual landmarks; she would have to get her bearings, so that she could find her way to her new home unassisted.

'Here we are!' said Agnieszka. 'I'll show you where you'll be living.'

They thanked the taxi driver and he helped Nia with her heavy suitcase, Nia followed Agnieszka into the lobby of a nearby high-rise building.

'Which floor is it?' asked Nia glancing at her suitcase.

'The top floor,' replied Agnieszka. 'Don't worry! We'll go up in the lift!'

The hallway of the building was stark and was painted in an olive green colour but the flat itself was a pleasant surprise and was clean and spacious.

'There are three bedrooms!' exclaimed Nia.

'Yes, two more teachers will be moving in shortly,' explained Agnieszka. 'I've already put some food in the fridge so that you can make yourself a snack.'

'Thank you so much!'

'I'll leave now because I'm sure that you must be very tired after your long journey but I'll see you here in the morning.'

'Thank you, I look forward to being shown around.'

Agnieszka left and the door clanked shut. Once Nia had been shown around Warsaw by Agnieszka, Nia planned to go and pay Marek a surprise visit. The thought of seeing him again made her smile.

Agnieszka was true to her word and the next morning, she arrived early to take Nia on a tour of Warsaw. Nia's flat was in the suburbs and in the light of day, Nia observed that lush greenery filled the gaps between the surrounding blocks of flats.

On her way to the tram stop, Nia noticed a few shops and a market. Agnieszka took Nia on the tram that Nia would need to catch each day to commute between her flat and the language school where she would be teaching English to adults. On the tram Nia noticed that the commuters were ready to give up their seat for anyone older even if they were not that much older and everyone was courteous.

Agnieszka gave Nia a tour of the language school and Nia met some of the female students. They were very chic and they were wearing pencil skirts in bright colours. Next, Agnieszka showed Nia around central Warsaw. In some of the main streets, there were shops selling luxuries but also retail outlets for pizzas and burgers. Street sellers attempted to sell their wares on the street corners. Picturesque buildings and quaint restaurants predominated, especially in the Old Town Square, and Nia was charmed.

Amongst other things, Agnieszka taught Nia how to order tea or *herbata* in Polish. Nia and Agnieszka sat outside a café near the Old Town Square, sipping a cup of tea. Nia had brought language books with her to Poland, but in addition, Agnieszka would be giving her Polish lessons at intervals and Nia would be giving the Polish students English lessons. Nia noticed that there were quite a few flower shops in central Warsaw. She saw a man carrying flowers and thought of Marek. Nia and Agnieszka didn't feel obliged to rush in and out of the café. When they were ready to go, they asked for the bill.

Nia caught the tram back to the suburbs and found a small grocery store and bakery near to the flat where she now lived. She bought some provisions including butter, cheese and tea bags at the grocery store.

Some items were cheaper than in the United Kingdom, some were the same price and some were more expensive. At the bakery, she purchased some bread.

When she went back to the flat, she decided that she would make herself some buttered bread and cheese followed by a cup of tea but to her disappointment, the butter turned out to be lard. She would have to learn the Polish word for butter!

In the afternoon, Nia used a map that Agnieszka had given her and found her way to Marek's flat in the centre of Warsaw. She was filled with excitement as she rang his doorbell.

Chapter 13

'Nia, my darling, what a wonderful surprise!' gasped Marek as he opened the door. 'When did you arrive?'

'Yesterday! I have a position as an English teacher, here in Warsaw,' said Nia enthusiastically. 'Also, I have a flat on the outskirts of Warsaw.'

'That's good news!' exclaimed Marek. 'I have to go to meet colleagues now but if you give me your address, I shall pick you up at your flat tonight at 7 pm and take you out to a restaurant.'

That evening, Marek arrived ten minutes earlier than arranged and knocked Nia's door. When she opened the door, Marek embraced her tightly and she smiled to herself.

He waited in the hallway while she quickly changed into a different outfit. Nia giggled to herself when she realized that she'd buttoned her cardigan incorrectly and the back of her skirt was tucked into her tights. However, she rearranged her skirt then undid the buttons on her cardigan and only kept Marek waiting a few minutes before they went to the restaurant.

'Have you been to this restaurant before?' asked Nia.

'Yes, I came here on the day after my name day celebration.'

'Your *name day*?'

'Yes, in Poland, people have a celebration on their name day: a day when everyone with a particular name celebrates and different names are celebrated on different days.'

They continued to chat and enjoyed the evening together. Nia felt certain that she had made the right decision by coming to Poland.

During Nia's first day at work, Marek joined her at the canteen at the language school so that they could have lunch together.

'What are you going to have today?' asked Marek as they queued in line.

'Everything on the menu is in Polish. I have learnt the words for the drinks but not the foods yet,' said Nia.

'Do you want me to translate?' asked Marek.

'No, I'm fine, I'm going to have pizza,' said Nia.

'Is that because you want pizza or because pizza is the only word that you recognize on the menu?'

'It is only my first day at the school,' laughed Nia.

They ordered two teas and paid for the food then Nia took the tray of food to a table whilst Marek waited for the teas. He brought the teas to the table where Nia was sitting.

'I've got you a tea,' said Marek as he placed two steaming mugs on the table.

'Thanks, I'll get some milk for the tea,' said Nia.

She darted to the counter and helped herself to a portion of milk assuming that this was included in the price of the tea as was the case in Britain. As she walked away, the woman at the till started shouting at Nia in Polish. Nia looked at Marek in dismay hoping that he would translate.

'You have to pay extra for the milk!' explained Marek.

'But in Britain, the milk is included in the price of the tea,' said Nia blushing. 'Perhaps you could explain on my behalf. Here's some money for the milk.'

'Don't worry!' said Marek.

Marek said something to the cashier who laughed and smiled towards Nia as he paid for the milk. Nia thanked him and took a bite of her pizza.

'Do you like your pizza?' asked Marek.

'Yes,' said Nia, 'but your fish, potatoes and coleslaw look even more delicious, I'll have that the next time!'

'Did you have a restful Sunday?' asked Marek.

'Not really, the washing machine flooded the bathroom and water went through the floor and the neighbours were complaining. The cold water had to be switched off and the landlord had to come and resolve the problem.'

'Do you have everything that you need?'

'Not quite, I need an umbrella and a tin opener.'

'Why didn't you bring an umbrella? Didn't you expect it to rain in Poland?'

'I imagined it cold but dry at this time of year,' said Nia laughing.

The following weekend, two colleagues Jane and Annette transferred from their flat into Nia's flat.

'Are you enjoying the teaching?' asked Annette.

'It's challenging but interesting,' said Nia. 'I'm in the process of working out what I can and can't afford on my teaching salary. Meals out are cheaper than in Britain but lots of things cost the same or more than in Britain.'

'Are you missing home?' asked Jane.

'Yes, I'm keeping in touch by letter and by phone but it's too expensive to phone too often,' said Nia.

'What do you think of the food in the canteen?' asked Jane.

'I love the omelette and the cabbage salad,' said Nia.

'Do you go to the school canteen every day?' asked Jane.

'Yes, I have been,' said Nia.

'Well we've discovered a lovely salad bar, we'll take you there next week,' said Annette.

'There's not so much choice in the local grocery store,' said Nia frowning.

'We've discovered a bigger supermarket,' said Annette excitedly. 'We'll take you there next week too.'

'How are you getting on with the Polish lessons?' asked Jane.

'I've only had a couple of lessons so far, the Polish teacher is lovely but Polish is very difficult, I can only remember the names of drinks and foods. The numbers seem impossible to remember!' declared Nia.

Nia was busy with her teaching and Marek worked long hours in his laboratory. However, they would snatch any opportunity to do something together. Nia was building up a collection of lovely memories to relate to her sisters when she next visited home. She would often have *naleśniki* (which means "pancakes" in English) with Marek on a Saturday. Sometimes, Marek and Nia would go to the cinema to see an American film with Polish subtitles. One weekend they went to see a piano recital in the open air in the park and visited the museum.

On another occasion, Nia and Marek took some days off and went to Prague together. Nia loved Prague too and noticed that there were some shops selling exquisite crystal chandeliers. The city centre had beautiful buildings.

They went to a restaurant together and Nia gazed out of the restaurant window. She watched the Czech business people walking briskly along the street wearing smart suit jackets in bright colours such as blue, green or purple.

When they returned to Warsaw, they were on a train with a corridor and individual compartments. This delighted Nia because she had only ever seen such trains in films.

Nia made progress with her Polish lessons and she liked her students, they were always enthusiastic and they were quick learners.

Winter arrived and there were lots of warm coats and hats on sale. Nearly everyone wore a hat and scarf. When the weather turned very cold, Nia started wearing additional layers of clothing including a thick vest and long socks underneath her boots and she began wearing her synthetic fur hat.

One evening, Marek and Nia went to see a ballet at the theatre. As they walked towards the theatre, Nia commented that the weather was very cold.

'You are stating the obvious!' exclaimed Marek.

'Well, if you think that I'm stating the obvious, you must have thought that everyone in Britain was stating the obvious all the time because they are always commenting on the weather!' said Nia.

They sat in a box with an excellent view of the stage. She was pleased that the two theatre tickets had cost much less than they would have done in Britain. The orchestra started and the ballerinas floated across the stage in their sparkling, swirling costumes. Marek reached across and held her hand firmly.

'I'm so glad to have you here with me,' he whispered to Nia.

'I'm happy to be here with you too,' she whispered.

She tried not to think about how much she missed meeting up with Anwen, Serena and the rest of her family. She was glad that she could speak to her family on the phone now and then. During her previous phone call, she had found out that Serena wasn't as enthusiastic about the work at the restaurant as Anwen but Serena had been delighted that she had managed to get some work as a singer at various venues in South Wales on the weekends. Nia thought how lovely it would be if she could find some way of splitting her time between the United Kingdom and Poland. No matter what the future held, she hoped that her future and Marek's future would be intertwined.

When Nia and Marek returned to Nia's flat after the ballet, Nia went into the kitchen to fill the small travel kettle that she had brought with her to make a cup of tea for them both. As she filled the kettle, Marek put his arms around her and kissed her hair and then the nape of her neck.

'I want you, Nia,' whispered Marek.

'I am so glad to be with you,' said Nia before Marek started to kiss her passionately. She didn't say how much she wanted to do more than just kiss.

'There is something I want to ask you,' said Marek.

At that point, the phone started to ring; its shrill and insistent tone beckoned Nia and prevented her from finding out what Marek wanted to ask. She darted into the hallway and grabbed the receiver.

At the other end of the phone, she recognized her father's voice immediately.

'Are you able to come back home at once?' her father asked.

'Why, what's wrong?' asked Nia starting to feel sick with worry.

'It's your grandmother, she's been taken ill and the doctors are not optimistic. Can you come back to see her?' her father pleaded.

'Yes, of course,' replied Nia.

'Thank you so much!' said her father.

'It was my father,' said Nia as she returned to the kitchen.

'Is there anything wrong?' asked Marek.

'My grandmother is ill, I have to go and see her,' replied Nia.

'But of course, you must go and see your grandmother!' insisted Marek before giving Nia a hug.

'I'll miss you but I have to go,' whispered Nia.

Chapter 14

Nia made the journey home and noticed many lights shining brightly in the darkness as her plane approached the airport in Britain.

Her sisters had made the trip to the airport with their mother and they all greeted her at the airport and hugged her tightly.

'How are you?' asked her mother.

'It's good to see you,' said Anwen.

'Think you've lost weight,' commented Serena.

When Nia arrived back in South Wales, she rushed to the hospital to see her grandmother and was shocked at how unwell her grandmother looked in comparison to the last time that she had seen her. Nia was sorry to have left her job in Poland and to be away from Marek but she knew that she had to spend time with her family for the time being and she wanted to visit her grandmother as often as possible. She spent some of the time working at the restaurant with her sisters.

A few weeks passed, during which time, the triplets visited their grandmother at the hospital as often as possible. On their twenty-third birthday, the triplets spent the afternoon at their grandmother's bedside.

Their grandmother seemed in better spirits that day. She wanted to hear all about Marek and asked Serena and Anwen if they'd met anyone special yet.

'We haven't had as much luck as Nia,' said Serena laughing.

'What sort of man would you like to marry then?' enquired their grandmother.

The triplets were relieved that their grandmother seemed more like her usual self and answered her probing questions.

'He's got to be intelligent, ethical and doing purposeful work,' said Nia and thought of Marek.

'He has to be kind and loyal,' said Anwen.

'He has to be attractive, fun and *passionate*,' responded Serena and laughed.

'I hope the fact that you've rushed back to Wales to see your grandmother won't cause problems between you and Marek,' said their grandmother as she peered at Nia.

'No, Marek is very understanding,' said Nia.

Nia declined to mention that she'd only received a few letters from Marek since she'd finished her job in Poland to spend some time with her grandmother. She didn't want to say anything negative so she forced herself to give as cheerful a smile as possible.

'It's lovely to see you three. It always makes me feel better,' said their grandmother.

'You'll be better and back home soon,' said Anwen.

The triplets kissed their grandmother and assured her that they would come and visit very soon. Their grandmother smiled and squeezed their hands.

'Don't forget, let me know if you've got any news,' said their grandmother and waved them goodbye.

However, shortly after that, the triplets' parents came home from a visit to the hospital and gave the triplets the news that their grandmother had passed away and a funeral had to be arranged. The triplets hugged their parents and each other.

'I told her she'd be better and back home soon,' said Anwen sadly.

On the day of their grandmother's funeral, the triplets arrived at the funeral parlour. As they entered the building, a few members of their family were already waiting in the majestic hallway. The triplets greeted them. As the triplets hugged various family members, the concentration of individuals in black garments made them sharply aware of the reality of the situation.

The protective wall they had built around themselves started to crack and they felt spears of pain strike them. Tears started to sting their eyes but they struggled to keep their composure.

They clambered into the funeral car in a daze and followed the hearse, which carried their grandmother's coffin. Serena, Nia and Anwen exchanged wide-eyed glances with one another, each one of them very aware of the pain that the other two were experiencing. At intervals, they took it in turns to reach across and squeeze one another's hands.

Although a part of them couldn't believe that the situation was real, another part of them knew that it was. They couldn't bear to focus upon the coffin being transported in the hearse in front as their car made the seemingly endless journey to the crematorium.

When the triplets arrived at the crematorium, a throng of mourners clad in black had already gathered outside. They glanced at the faces and recognized other members of their family amongst the crowd. Waves of sadness surged over them again and once again, they struggled to keep their composure.

However, they were comforted by the fact that so many people had turned up to mourn with them. Even the heavy grey clouds seemed to be mourning and looked ready to deluge them with tears of rain.

They filed into the crematorium behind the coffin, which was laden with an abundance of pink roses. Their grandmother had loved the colour pink, it had appeared on her china, wallpaper, curtains and bedspread. Likewise, she had loved wearing the colour pink and she had owned numerous pink garments including a pink cotton apron. She had been delighted that Anwen liked that colour too.

During the service, the eulogy was given and moving tributes to their dear grandmother were made. Tears streamed down the triplets' cheeks.

However, as anecdotes about their grandmother's kindness and generosity were told, they smiled beneath their tears feeling blessed to have had her unconditional love, which had warmed their lives like the sun warms the earth. Without their grandmother, the world seemed like a colder place.

The triplets struggled to sing the final hymn. In contrast to the organ music, their voices trailed off and they dabbed their eyes. Even though, Serena was a singer by profession on a part-time basis in addition to her work at her father's restaurant, she felt too sad to keep singing that day.

At the end of the service, they shuffled outside and stood in line as the other mourners filed passed and offered hugs and words of condolence.

There were distant members of the family there that they hadn't seen for years. In the midst of their sadness, the triplets felt heartened to receive their hugs.

'I am sorry for your loss, it's a pity we don't have more time to meet up with loved ones more often when life is so short,' commented Mr Williams before starting to sob very loudly and then disappearing into the throng of people clad in black.

'We'll have to meet up more often, we only meet up for weddings and funerals now,' was repeated throughout the day.

The triplets clambered back into the funeral car for the journey to a nearby hotel for the funeral reception. A buffet had been prepared. Cups of tea were served. They had the opportunity to chat to close family, distant relatives and friends and to share memories of their grandmother.

Although their grandmother had played different roles to different people, she was remembered affectionately by everyone who had known her.

Part way through the buffet, a tall man in a smart black suit with auburn hair and green eyes came over to talk to the triplets and offer his condolences. Nia, Anwen and Serena stared up at him trying to identify him.

Then Nia realized who he was; it was Owen, her beloved childhood friend. She used his name casually letting him think that she'd known his identity all along. She was pleased that he was unaware of her initial lack of recognition. In her defence, Nia hadn't seen Owen since childhood and he had grown into a handsome young man. He was tall with broad shoulders and a warm smile.

'I find it difficult to tell the difference between the three of you but you're Nia, aren't you? I can tell because you're wearing the brooch that I bought you when we were children. We'll have to meet up for coffee sometime,' suggested Owen. 'I'm an artist now. You always wanted to become a scientist, didn't you? Did you go into that field?'

'Yes, I did do a degree in biochemistry and a Master of Science degree and I'm hoping to get work related to that in due course. It would be lovely to meet up with you for coffee.'

Nia decided that it was not relevant at that point to mention that she was dating someone in Poland.

'I'm sorry that we are meeting under such sad circumstances,' said Owen looking crestfallen but he quickly regained his composure and added, 'I can remember your grandmother visiting you when we were children.'

The rest of the day passed uneventfully, the triplets went back to their parents' house for a cup of tea.

'It was lovely to see family and friends that we haven't seen for ages but it's a pity that we only have the chance to meet up with some of our family and friends on sad occasions such as a funeral,' said Anwen.

'I'm going upstairs to change,' declared their father. 'I'm going to put this black suit in the suitcase on top of the wardrobe. I don't want to see it every time I open the wardrobe and be reminded of today and the loss of my mother.'

Due to the cost, Nia didn't usually phone Marek, she usually wrote to him instead but after the funeral, Nia tried to phone Marek to let him know of the loss of her grandmother but an unknown woman answered.

'Please could I speak to Marek?' asked Nia politely.

'Marek has moved out and I live here now,' announced the female voice.

'Do you happen to have Marek's new phone number and address please?'

'Sorry, I do not have any information.'

'Does he come back to the flat at all to check for mail?'

'No, Marek has moved out and I live here now,' repeated the woman.

Nia tried contacting the university that she'd attended to see if she could find out Marek's contact details at work, via the research team in the United Kingdom but it appeared that Marek had taken up a new position in Poland and no one was able to provide her with his new work address. Nia was unable to contact Marek but he knew her details so she felt devastated that she'd received no phone calls or letters from him. She kept thinking about him but realized that she had no way of finding out where he had gone.

Chapter 15

Nia knew that she was in love with Marek. She had thought that he was in love with her too. Why hadn't he been in touch?

However, Nia wanted to get a scientific post and so turned her attention to applying for appropriate positions in the area. She decided to apply for a position working in a laboratory in her hometown and succeeded in getting through the interview. She had a scientific background so it was a logical progression. As always, she threw herself into her work and this did help because it meant that she didn't have quite so much time to dwell on why she hadn't heard from Marek.

All three of the triplets were working and they made the decision to rent a conveniently located house together. The triplets enjoyed sharing a house. They were pleased that they were able to split the cost of rent and bills between them. They knew that being able to share the costs was a great advantage and reduced the costs that they would have incurred if they had rented separate houses. In addition, splitting the household chores between them saved time in comparison to the longer times they felt sure would have been required to keep up with everything if they had rented a house each.

They developed a smooth routine. They all got up at 7 am and had toast or cereal. Anwen and Serena usually made breakfast because they left the house later than Nia in the mornings.

However, one morning, Anwen left for work earlier than usual. She was walking to the restaurant when a car slowed and pulled up to the kerb next to Anwen. The man driving rolled down his window and leaned towards the open window.

'Get in!' he urged.

Anwen's heart pounded. Why was a stranger asking her to get into his car? It was pouring with rain and there was nobody around. Anwen ignored the man and crossed the road briskly. She started to walk in the opposite direction to the car.

When Anwen met up with Nia at lunch time, she told her about the disconcerting event.

'Yes,' said Nia, 'I already know about it because it was my boss trying to give *me* a lift to the laboratory but mistaking you for me.'

'Oh dear!' exclaimed Anwen. 'Was he offended when I ignored him?'

'No, don't worry. I did explain that it must have been you on your way to work and that you wouldn't have known that he was my boss,' replied Nia.

The triplets were able to celebrate their twenty-fourth birthday together at their new house. However, they were painfully aware that a year ago, they had been able to celebrate with their grandmother and now that was no longer possible.

Nia was chided by her sisters if she happened to mention how much she missed Marek.

'Love at first sight is a myth,' insisted Anwen. 'You should give other people a chance and feelings might grow.'

'I am trying not to think about Marek,' insisted Nia unconvincingly.

'Well that's good, you really need to stop thinking about what's his name and move on,' advised Serena. 'Marek probably isn't thinking about you and could be married with a child on the way by now.'

Nia got on well with her colleagues. However, she hadn't agreed to go on any dates with anyone. She found herself comparing everyone to Marek.

If they didn't look, talk and act like Marek – and of course, no one did – they didn't capture her interest.

However, she kept these thoughts to herself. Her family and friends wouldn't approve if they realized quite how much she was still tormented with thoughts about him.

The triplets had transported all of their things from their parents' house to their rented house so at intervals they would spend time sorting through and organizing their stuff. One day, Nia walked in on Serena as she was sorting through family photographs. Serena was detaching the photographs from several old albums and carefully putting them inside a new album in chronological order. Strewn across Serena's bed were all the photographs that she had discarded; the photographs of the identical triplets during the periods when one of them was affected by hypothyroidism and they didn't look like identical triplets.

'Look, I've edited the album!' exclaimed Serena proudly. 'We look like identical triplets throughout the album now.'

'But you can't edit history!' exclaimed Nia. 'The hypothyroidism was part of our childhood experience; you can't edit it out as if it never happened.'

'But now the three of us look slim and identical in every photo,' stated Serena defiantly.

'Come on! We have to put the photos that you discarded back into the new album,' said Nia firmly.

'But if we make new friends or have a boyfriend, we can show them the new, edited album without feeling embarrassed or having to explain about having hypothyroidism during childhood,' pleaded Serena.

'Well, we are keeping all of the photos, and besides if you and Anwen hadn't been available for comparison, my childhood hypothyroidism might not have been picked up and if you and I hadn't been available for comparison, Anwen's childhood hypothyroidism might not have been picked up either!'

'And if you and Anwen hadn't been available for comparison, my childhood hypothyroidism might never have been picked up,' added Serena with a shudder.

'The photos might be useful in the future! You never know! So we're keeping all of the photos,' insisted Nia.

One Friday, the triplets arranged to meet each other for lunch. When they reached the café, they ordered jacket potatoes with tuna, sweet corn and mayonnaise and three cups of very milky coffee then sat down to chat whilst waiting for their order to be brought to their table.

Anwen expressed how much she enjoyed working at the restaurant and developing recipes in her spare time but Serena made it obvious that she was a little bit fed up of working at the restaurant to say the least.

'I've just got to do something different. I don't think I can stand working at the restaurant much longer. It's just not what I want to do with my life!' declared Serena in a dramatic way.

'What would you like to do?' enquired Nia.

'As you know I've been doing some work as a singer on a part-time basis but I want to work exclusively as a singer and musician!' announced Serena.

'That would be good,' agreed Anwen.

'Well, I wanted to be a research scientist,' complained Nia.

'Why are you moaning?' asked Serena. 'You do work in a laboratory.'

'Yes, but I'm not involved in a research project,' said Nia.

'Well, what do you think of this?' asked Serena and pointed her beautifully manicured finger at an advertisement for a position as a singer on a cruise ship. 'On the basis of my part-time experience, I think I stand a good chance.'

Their food arrived and Serena quickly slipped the advertisement back into her compact handbag.

'It does sound quite exciting,' said Anwen. 'But what about us? If you do get this position, you'll be leaving and it's only been a few months since we all got the house together and what does Dad think about you leaving the restaurant?'

'I'd still see you at intervals. I haven't told Dad yet. I don't need to say anything unless I know that my application has been successful,' replied Serena.

'Oh, don't worry about us. Anyway, Serena can write and we can meet up at intervals, we could join her for cruises!' said Nia not wanting to dampen Serena's enthusiasm.

That evening, when Serena returned home, she applied for the position on the cruise ship. She would have to wait and see if she would be successful.

Chapter 16

During the weeks that followed since Serena had applied to work on a cruise ship, she was impatient to find out what mail had arrived each day. As soon as Serena heard the sound of envelopes being put through their letterbox each morning, she'd rush to check the mail.

'Bills or junk mail, nothing interesting,' she said to herself most days.

However, one morning a few weeks after she'd submitted her application, a white envelope came through the letterbox and the neatly handwritten name and address on the envelope caught Serena's attention. She tore open the envelope eagerly and began reading the letter.

The instruction for her to report to Southampton caught her attention as she glanced through the letter. Her application had led to an audition, which was successful, and a job offer followed. Things seemed to happen quickly after that and within a few more weeks, Serena received an invitation to commence her new job on a cruise ship.

A few weeks later, Serena was packing her possessions and rushing to catch the appropriate train so that she was early for her meeting with her new manager.

Serena soon settled into life on the cruise ship. After she had been on various cruise ships for many months, Anwen and Nia joined her on one cruise so that the triplets could celebrate their twenty-fifth birthday together.

The triplets spent some of the time on-board doing things together and some of the time doing separate activities. On the first day at sea, at the start of the evening, Serena gave a concert and Anwen attended a talk at the on-board art gallery. Nia spent the time in the on-board library.

However, later that evening, they had planned to meet one another to celebrate their birthday together.

While Serena was standing on deck waiting to meet her sisters, she caught the attention of one of the passengers. He had black hair and dark brown eyes. He came over to talk to Serena. Serena was wearing a black shift dress, a striking red pendant and black high-heeled shoes. Her fingernails were neatly painted with red nail varnish and she wore elaborate red earrings and deep red lipstick. Her long hair fell around her shoulders.

'Hi, I'm Adrian, are you enjoying yourself on this cruise?'

'Yes thank you. What are you planning to do next tonight?' asked Serena politely.

'I haven't decided yet,' responded Adrian. 'I'll have to take another look at the programme of events.'

'Yes, there's plenty going on,' commented Serena.

Before leaving, Adrian said that he hoped to see her again. Just after he had left, Anwen and Nia joined Serena and the three of them celebrated their birthday together.

The next evening, the triplets met at Serena's cabin to get ready for a party hosted by the captain of the ship.

'I haven't got much make-up with me, is it okay if I borrow some of your eye shadow?' asked Nia.

'Of course,' muttered Serena.

'I don't often bother to wear eye shadow,' said Nia as she proceeded to put some eye shadow on her eyelids. 'How does it look?'

'The way that you've applied your eye shadow doesn't look right and it's given your eyelids an *inflamed* look,' gasped Serena, 'I'll re-do it for you!'

Serena finished applying Nia's make-up. In addition, Serena let her sisters borrow her evening gowns. Serena wore a red satin dress, Nia wore a sapphire blue silk gown and Anwen wore a cerise chiffon dress. After getting ready, they entered the party together.

The next evening, Serena attended a private backstage party for the entertainment staff. One of Serena's colleagues was sure that Serena and a fellow on-board musician named Michael would get on really well together and told Serena that she was going to introduce her to him.

Serena's colleague tugged on Serena's sleeve and said, 'Serena come and meet Michael.'

Michael had grey eyes, brown hair and a moustache.

Serena walked towards him, her head held high, and introduced herself. 'Are you enjoying the cruise so far Michael?'

'Yes Serena, it's wonderful and it's so lovely to have the opportunity to talk to you,' said Michael, 'I have heard so much about you from your colleague. I enjoyed the songs that you sang at your concert earlier. You have a wonderful voice. Do you write your own songs?'

'Yes, I do sometimes; I enjoy writing songs.'

'I've written some songs myself recently, would you like to see them sometime and tell me what you think?'

'Yes, I'd love to.'

'I hope you'll like them.'

'I'm sure that I'll love them!' said Serena.

As Serena talked, she felt aware that Michael appeared to be listening intently to everything that she said. They spent the rest of the evening chatting to each other.

'Would you like to join me for a meal tomorrow?' asked Michael at the end of the evening.

'Yes thank you, that would be great!' replied Serena.

'At which restaurant shall we meet tomorrow evening?' asked Michael.

'Well there are plenty to choose from, there are millions of them well not millions but at least a dozen of them,' said Serena and laughed.

'We could go to the staff restaurant. It has a lovely view of the sea,' said Michael.

'Yes, that sounds good,' responded Serena.

'Great!' said Michael and he gave Serena a hug and a light kiss on her cheek before he left.

The next day, Serena and Michael met as arranged. Serena was wearing a deep purple shift dress, which suited her and her hair fell around her shoulders. He looked at Serena admiringly and told her that she looked beautiful.

They talked about films and books that they liked and places that they'd visited. He asked Serena lots of questions. She was beginning to enjoy his company. He seemed to be very knowledgeable about any topic that they discussed.

Serena agreed to spend the next afternoon with Michael and was still in a rush to get ready when he knocked on her cabin door. They both decided to go to the staff restaurant for afternoon tea. They shared a pot of tea and they had freshly baked scones whilst chatting animatedly to each other. They talked about their ambitions for the future as they enjoyed the view of the glistening blue sea.

During the evenings, after her concerts, Serena would go back to Michael's cabin and they would sit on deck chairs on the balcony of his cabin gazing at the scenery as the ship sailed across the serene Mediterranean Sea towards the next destination.

Serena and Michael met up with each other as often as possible and on one occasion, they reminisced about childhood holidays. Michael was also based in Wales and they discovered that they had both spent time at the same beach when they were younger.

'I can never resist walking across the sand when I visit the beach during the summer and I usually end up with shoes full of sand,' admitted Serena.

They both chatted about how they used to spend summers when they were children. Michael used to go camping with his parents.

Nia and Anwen didn't see Serena as much as they had expected on the cruise due to her having rehearsals and work and meeting up with Michael in the areas of the ship for staff only.

However, they still loved being on the cruise ship; there were so many opportunities to dress up in evening gowns. Anwen and Nia's clothes didn't seem to be sophisticated enough for all of the events but Serena was happy to share her wardrobe with them.

During the cruise, Nia spent most of the time sitting on the balcony of her cabin with a book borrowed from the library or at the on-board gym exercising. Reading a book was her favourite way of relaxing and working out at the gym was her favourite way of exercising.

Because Nia liked to chill out with a book or attend the gym and Serena was often occupied, Anwen attended many events on her own.

During one of the talks that Anwen attended, Anwen borrowed Serena's black shift dress, red pendant and black high-heeled shoes. She also wore matching red lipstick.

Anwen noticed that a young man with black hair and dark brown eyes was occasionally glancing in her direction. Anwen liked the look of him. She smiled at him and he blushed slightly. They continued to exchange glances and at the end of the talk, he took the opportunity to come and chat to her.

'Hi!' said the young man. 'It's lovely to see you again.'

'See me again?' repeated Anwen with a puzzled expression on her face.

'Yes, I saw you on the first day at sea. My name's Adrian and I'm accompanying my mother on this cruise.'

'That's so sweet of you.'

On another day, Anwen came across Adrian at one of the cafés on the ship and they began chatting and decided to have a coffee together.

Whilst they drank their cup of coffee, Adrian looked intently at Anwen as he spoke, 'Have you been on a cruise before?'

'No, this is the first time, my two sisters are on the cruise too,' responded Anwen without bothering to explain that she was one of identical triplets because she was impatient to find out more about Adrian. 'What about you?'

'I've been on several cruises, I've visited Italy, France and also Norway and Iceland, it really is a wonderful way to travel and see the world!'

'Yes, I've enjoyed every minute and I'd definitely love to come on a ship again. I think I'll try to stow away on the last day and stay on the ship a bit longer!' said Anwen jokingly.

Adrian smiled and his dark brown eyes sparkled as he asked, 'Where do you live?'

'I live in South Wales not far from the sea.'

'That sounds great!'

'Yes, the scenery is spectacular and in the town where I live, there are many wonderful cafés and restaurants. In fact, I work in a restaurant that is owned by my father. It's a lovely restaurant.'

'I'd love to visit the restaurant at some time and see the beautiful scenery that you've mentioned.'

'You'd love South Wales,' said Anwen. 'Where do you live?'

'The south of England, I have a dental practice there,' replied Adrian.

Anwen smiled at Adrian. He was very easy to talk to and she felt comfortable with him.

On another occasion, they met up at the art gallery and they started chatting to each other again as if they'd known each other much longer than they had.

'What do you like doing in your spare time?' asked Adrian.

'I enjoy developing new recipes in my spare time, what about you?'

'Swimming, that's been my hobby for as long as I can remember,' responded Adrian before quizzing Anwen on her taste in music and books.

They lost track of the time and chatted for a few hours. They were surprised when they realized how much time had elapsed.

'I hope that we meet up again soon! I very much enjoy your company!' said Adrian.

'So do I!' said Anwen then went to meet Nia and Serena for supper.

'I'm having a wonderful time with Michael,' said Serena. 'It's a pity that you don't have much luck with men Anwen, perhaps I should try to think of some tips to pass on to you.'

Serena was unaware that Anwen had been talking to Adrian but to avoid making Serena feel awkward about her comment, Anwen decided to refrain from mentioning her encounters with Adrian to Serena or Nia.

On another day, Anwen saw Adrian sitting by one of the pools and they spent the afternoon talking to one another. Adrian attempted to pay Anwen many compliments.

Anwen and Adrian discussed a range of topics in more depth: the foods that they liked and disliked; their taste in music; their taste in books; their taste in films; the destinations that they'd visited and what they enjoyed doing in their spare time.

They also discussed the things that they felt passionate about and the things about their lives that they wished that they could change. Their tastes were similar.

Furthermore, they seemed to laugh at the same things. Anwen had a quirky sense of humour that most people didn't get but Adrian seemed to like her sense of humour and turn of phrase.

The next evening, Anwen and Adrian went to a cocktail party that was taking place on the ship. They seemed to have a rapport and didn't run out of topics of conversation. Then Adrian held Anwen in his arms as they danced with each other.

On the penultimate evening of the cruise, Adrian escorted Anwen back to the deck on which her cabin was located and gave her a gentle kiss on the lips.

'I'd like to see you again after this holiday,' said Adrian as he looked at Anwen and smiled.

'That would be lovely!' replied Anwen rapidly.

'Good, that's decided then, let's meet up tomorrow evening at 9 pm at the same place as tonight and we'll make a point of swapping our contact details so that we can keep in touch,' said Adrian.

'I look forward to seeing you tomorrow,' replied Anwen.

'Me too,' said Adrian.

On the last night of the cruise, Serena was invited to dine with Michael at one of the main restaurants rather than the staff restaurant. Serena wore her black shift dress, red pendant and black high-heeled shoes and she wore matching red lipstick.

Serena and Michael began the meal with sumptuous garlic mushrooms followed by baked salmon and ended the meal with some coffee. When they were drinking their coffee, Michael pushed a little box towards Serena, which promptly slid across the table and fell onto the floor. Serena picked it up and looked at Michael.

'What's this?' asked Serena.

'Well open it and find out!' said Michael eagerly.

Serena opened the box to reveal an exquisite engagement ring.

'I know that we haven't known each other for long but I feel as if I've known you all my life. Will you marry me?' asked Michael.

Serena looked at him in surprise and then glanced at the ring, 'Yes! Yes! I know we haven't known each other for long but I feel the same way. Thank you for this ring. It's gorgeous!' exclaimed Serena as she tried on the ring and admired the ring on her finger.

At that moment, Adrian approached the table. He rushed towards Serena but had his back to Michael.

'Hello, my darling, I'm going to miss you when this cruise is over,' he said.

'What's going on?' asked Michael.

Adrian glanced behind, saw Michael and became flustered.

'Have you been meeting up with both of us?' asked Michael.

'No, of course not!' exclaimed Serena.

'I'm sorry, I'll leave,' said Adrian. 'I'm so sorry!'

He seemed to be glancing at the ring on Serena's finger and looked bewildered as he rushed away.

'I believe he talked to me once at the start of the cruise but I haven't been meeting up with him throughout the cruise!' said Serena.

'Well, why did he say that he'd miss you?' asked Michael.

'I don't know, perhaps, he's been talking to Anwen or Nia and thought that I was one of them, it wouldn't be the first time that has happened but they haven't mentioned anything about talking to anyone in particular.'

'Yes, it is possible that he mistook you for Anwen or Nia. Perhaps I overreacted but I've been rehearsing my romantic speech for the evening all day and I didn't want anything to spoil things.'

'Don't worry. The evening hasn't been spoilt and the evening is not over yet!' said Serena.

Michael held Serena's hand and Serena started to imagine herself wearing a white satin wedding dress and pictured herself being showered with multi-coloured confetti.

Elsewhere on the ship, Anwen sat in the bar where she had arranged to meet Adrian. She had arrived at 8.45 pm and had found herself a seat with a view of the entrance. She glanced towards the entrance at regular intervals. At 9 pm, Adrian had not arrived as planned.

Five minutes passed. Ten minutes passed. Half an hour passed. An hour later Anwen decided that Adrian was not coming. She was worried about him. She didn't know why he was late and she didn't know his cabin number. She hoped that he would suddenly appear and apologize for the delay.

After ordering another coffee and glancing at her magazine for another half an hour, Anwen admitted to herself that it didn't look as if Adrian was going to come. She put her magazine into her bag and looked around one last time before she was obliged to walk back to her cabin.

Re-living every wonderful memory of Adrian in her mind made her feel disappointed at the thought of experiencing such a lovely time with him and then possibly not seeing him again.

Later that evening, Serena and Nia burst into Anwen's cabin. Serena shared her happy news about her engagement to Michael. However, in her excitement, Serena forgot to mention Adrian's appearance during the occasion and Anwen didn't want to cast a shadow over Serena's special evening by mentioning that she had met someone too but he hadn't turned up for their date.

Chapter 17

When Serena came home for a week's holiday, following the cruise, Serena was able to tell the rest of her family about her whirlwind romance and engagement to Michael. Serena also took Michael to meet her parents who were chatty and warm towards him. On meeting Michael, her father seemed to approve of him. When Michael had the opportunity, he took Serena to meet his parents whose cat even made Serena welcome by curling up on Serena's lap and refusing to move.

Following the funeral of the triplets' grandmother, Nia and Owen had remained in touch. They met up for coffee at regular intervals. After the cruise with Anwen and Serena, Nia arranged to meet Owen again.

'Do you remember all the fun we used to have when we used to meet up when we were children?' asked Owen.

'Yes, we had lots of fun!' agreed Nia. 'We were always the best of friends.'

'I haven't said anything until now but I hope that one day we will become more than friends.'

'I'm flattered,' said Nia. 'But shall we stay as friends for now and see how things go?'

However, their friendship grew and they would talk to one another on the phone every day and then on the weekends, they would go out for meals together.

One day, Nia was surprised to receive a delivery of red roses. Nia read the label, which said:

Dear Nia,
Would you like to go out on a date with me?
Love Owen

Later that evening, Owen rang Nia, 'Did you get the flowers that I sent you?'

'Yes, I did thank you, they are beautiful!' exclaimed Nia.

'What's your response to my note? Would you like to go out on a date with me?

'Yes, I would like to go on a date with you, that would be lovely,' replied Nia.

'I can't believe you've agreed,' exclaimed Owen.

On their first proper date, Owen took Nia to a restaurant overlooking the beach. After they'd had a delicious meal, Owen held Nia's hand.

'I love being with you Nia,' said Owen.

'Thank you, I'm happy to be here with you tonight too. But let's take things slowly,' said Nia as she fidgeted with her necklace.

'Okay,' agreed Owen.

'But I do like the way that you ring me when you say you are going to ring me, you make me feel that I can rely on you,' added Nia.

For a long time Nia had remained convinced that Marek would get back in touch but that hadn't happened. Nia still thought of Marek and the way that he had made her feel.

However, as time passed, she became certain that she must have been mistaken about Marek's feelings for her and that he hadn't really loved her after all. Perhaps another woman had appeared on the scene.

Nia had been so heartbroken following the ending of her relationship with Marek that she feared getting hurt like that again.

However, Owen's words and actions were definitely increasing her levels of trust in him and her belief that something wonderful could work out between the two of them.

Nia had felt that Marek had been perfect for her but if she couldn't be with Marek, she wanted him to be as happy as possible even if that meant that he was with someone new. She had to try to find happiness herself, without Marek.

The following week, Nia had the house to herself. Serena was away working on the cruise ship and Anwen was visiting their parents. Nia invited Owen for a meal. She made risotto. When Owen arrived at the expected time, Nia served the risotto.

After the risotto, a fruit salad and a coffee, Owen said that he had better walk home. Before leaving, he leant forward and kissed her on the lips.

She couldn't deny that she had feelings for Owen. However, she had fallen deeply in love with Marek only to be disappointed so she promised herself that she wouldn't allow herself to fall so deeply in love again.

She had made herself too vulnerable and then it had been painful when things hadn't worked out. However, she enjoyed Owen's kiss and responded to it, despite her previous misgivings.

Several weeks after the cruise, Anwen had persuaded Nia and her mother to meet up with her so that they could go shopping together and then go somewhere for a cup of coffee.

The day was a success. Their mother persuaded Anwen to try on a deep pink shift dress, which wasn't the usual sort of thing that Anwen wore.

'That dress suits you,' said Nia.

'You've got to get it!' urged their mother so Anwen took their advice and purchased the dress.

Then they went to a café for a cup of coffee and Anwen decided to confide in her mother and Nia about her ill-fated romance with Adrian.

Anwen went into more detail about the events on the cruise ship and explained that she hadn't mentioned anything earlier because Serena had been so cheerful that she hadn't wanted to cast a shadow over things by moaning.

'*Anwen*,' said Nia, 'I just remembered something that Serena mentioned to me that may be very relevant to you.'

'What have you remembered?' asked Anwen.

'Serena told me that just after she'd got engaged and was wearing the engagement ring from Michael, a man appeared.'

'Who was the man?' asked Anwen.

'Well, someone with whom she'd talked briefly at the start of the cruise came over to her and told her that he would miss her when the cruise was over. Serena was puzzled but when he saw her engagement ring, he apologized and disappeared,' said Nia.

'It must have been Adrian and he must have mistaken Serena for me,' said Anwen rapidly. 'He must have thought that *I was engaged* to Michael and therefore, he decided to keep out of the way, do you think?'

'Yes, that must be it!' exclaimed Nia.

'What shall I do now?' asked Anwen as she gripped Nia's arm…

Chapter 18

'I know the name of the village where Adrian lives and I know that he has a dental practice there so if I go to his village, I should be able to find him! I'm going to get the train there and I'm going to locate the dental practice and find Adrian and explain everything,' continued Anwen.

'Yes, you do that!' said Nia. 'I'll come with you if I can get the time off work and then you'll have company and moral support.'

Nia let Anwen know that she would be able to get time off work. Therefore, Anwen booked a twin room at the bed and breakfast located in the village where Adrian lived. She also purchased train tickets for herself and Nia.

Anwen wished that Adrian had given her the chance to explain any misunderstanding because although she'd mentioned that she had two sisters, she hadn't explained that she was one of identical triplets. Without that knowledge, Adrian would have just assumed that Serena was Anwen because they were so similar in appearance.

Anwen felt more jubilant than she had felt since the day that Adrian hadn't turned up. She was hopeful that she could not only find Adrian within the next few days but also explain everything.

The train journey wasn't monotonous because Anwen and Nia were able to sit next to each other and chat throughout the journey.

They arrived at Adrian's village and checked into their accommodation. The owner of the bed and breakfast was particularly friendly and chatty. She showed Nia and Anwen to their room and asked them many questions. She seemed to be trying to find out everything about them including why they were visiting the area. Anwen wasn't going to explain the reason for their visit so provided vague answers.

After putting their overnight bags in their room, Nia and Anwen walked into the village and found a quaint looking café where they decided to have lunch. There were embroidered tablecloths on each table. On each tablecloth there was a little vase containing pink roses. Nia and Anwen looked at the menu and ordered a sandwich and a mug of hot chocolate.

'The dental practice is at the other end of the village,' said Anwen as she sipped her drink, 'so after lunch we could walk there and see what happens.'

'If you want, I'll stay here and you can meet me back here,' Nia offered.

'Okay, that's a good idea actually and I shouldn't be too long,' agreed Anwen.

Anwen gave Nia a hug before leaving the café and walking towards the other end of the village. She found her way to the dental practice. She took a deep breath and then pushed the heavy door open and entered the building. She walked to the reception desk. There was no option; she would have to ask a member of staff about Adrian.

'Excuse me but is Adrian here today?'

'Adrian's not at work today,' replied the man at the reception desk.

'Thanks,' muttered Anwen barely able to conceal her disappointment.

'He'll be back in work tomorrow morning,' said the man with a very wide smile.

'Thank you, thanks for your help!' said Anwen thinking that the man would be wondering who she was. She rushed back to the café where Nia was waiting.

'What happened?' asked Nia as soon as Anwen appeared.

'Well, Adrian wasn't there today but...'

'Go on,' interrupted Nia.

'But, he should be back at the dental practice tomorrow, assuming that it is the same Adrian.'

'We'll get up early tomorrow and you can visit the dental practice as soon as we've had breakfast,' said Nia.

'Thanks for coming with me,' said Anwen. 'I'll have time to call in at the dental practice in the morning before we catch the train home in the afternoon.'

The sisters went for a walk to a nearby park. Anwen hoped that she would be able to speak to Adrian the next day so that she could explain everything.

Later, they returned to the café and they had scrambled egg on toast followed by a pot of tea for two.

'So far, so good,' said Nia to Anwen as Anwen poured tea from a little white china teapot with a floral pattern on one side.

That night, Anwen kept Nia awake until late by talking about Adrian.

The next morning, Anwen woke up to the sound of her portable alarm clock.

'Are you awake?' Anwen whispered to Nia.

'Not quite,' muttered Nia and continued to lie in her comfortable bed.

Anwen on the other hand tiptoed out of bed and managed to work out how to operate the shower. Once Anwen had dressed, she made her bed and urged Nia to get up.

'I want to go and have breakfast soon,' whispered Anwen.

'Just counting to twenty,' replied Nia.

Anwen got up to look out of the window and tapped her fingers against the windowsill. Nia sat up and stretched her arms. Nia yawned and as if in slow motion made her way to the *en suite* bathroom and splashed water on her face.

'Give me ten minutes and I'll be ready and we can go down for breakfast together, is that okay?' asked Nia.

'Yes, fine, that's great!' said Anwen and made sure that she handed Nia anything that she might need to try to speed up the process.

After initial reluctance, it was not long before Nia was ready to join Anwen for breakfast. The sisters went downstairs and found their way to the dining room. They were given some triangular slices of toast in a toast rack and tea in a silver-coloured teapot.

Anwen picked up the teapot and poured tea into two cups for her and Nia. Anwen seemed to be eating everything as rapidly as possible as if time would pass more quickly, the more quickly that she did things. Nia was staring slightly blankly at an oil painting hanging neatly on the dining room wall.

As soon as the sisters had finished their breakfast, they went back to their room. Nia said that she would read her book in the room while Anwen walked to the dental practice. Prior to leaving, Anwen gave her hair another brush as she looked at herself earnestly in the mirror.

After saying goodbye to Nia, Anwen left the room and walked briskly along the pavement, enjoying the feel of a slightly cold breeze blowing against her face. On reaching the dental practice, she took a deep breath before pushing open the door. As she entered, the familiar smell of the same cleaning agents that dentists everywhere seemed to use filled her nostrils. The smell usually filled her with trepidation because she associated it with the wait to see a dentist to find out whether or not treatment was required or to have treatment. However, that day, she felt a surge of excitement. As she walked towards the reception desk, she saw Adrian walking into the room from another entrance carrying a pile of files.

'Surprised to see me?' she asked...

Chapter 19

Adrian glanced towards Anwen and then he dropped the files onto the floor and kneeled down to pick them up whilst at the same time looking up at her.

'What are you doing here? Where's your fiancé?' asked Adrian with an extremely puzzled expression on his face, confirming Anwen's suspicion that he had mistaken Serena for her.

'I haven't got a fiancé. My sister Serena got engaged to Michael on the last night of the cruise and you mistook my sister Serena for me!' explained Anwen.

'What do you mean?' asked Adrian.

'Well I told you that I had two sisters but what I didn't mention was that we are identical triplets and my sisters and I look very much alike, people often muddle us up. Sometimes, people are not sure which one of us is which!' Anwen finished her explanation and stared at Adrian waiting for his response.

Adrian laughed and then walked up to Anwen and gave her a hug and kissed her on the lips, much to the astonishment of an elderly woman sitting in the waiting room adjacent to the reception desk.

'Thanks for explaining everything to me!' said Adrian with a tone of appreciation in his voice.

'I know you've got to get back to work now and I've got a train to catch but does this mean we can carry on meeting up with each other?' asked Anwen breathlessly.

'Yes, yes, of course, definitely!' said Adrian. 'If you give me your number, I'll ring you later to check you are back home okay and we can arrange to meet up as soon as possible!'

After exchanging details, Anwen waved goodbye and almost floated back to the bed and breakfast to describe the morning's events to Nia.

'Did you see Adrian?' asked Nia as soon as Anwen entered their room.

'Yes, I did and he had assumed that Serena was me and that Michael was my fiancé but I've explained it all and everything is okay now and we're back in touch with each other. I can't describe how happy I feel!' said Anwen triumphantly as she gave Nia a hug.

Later, they had to pack their bags and make their way to the train station. However, the journey had been worthwhile. Anwen smiled to herself when she remembered that she would be speaking to Adrian that evening. They caught their train and Anwen chatted happily to Nia as the train headed back towards South Wales.

Nia and Owen had been dating for nearly a year. Nia was no longer tormenting herself with unanswered questions about Marek. She no longer had that sinking feeling in her stomach when she remembered the way things had ended with Marek and she felt boosted by the way that things seemed to be progressing with Owen who was very attentive towards her. However, Nia had tried to hide her amusement when on one occasion, he had greeted Serena with a kiss and claimed afterwards that he had mistaken Serena for Nia and on another occasion, he had given Anwen a hug and then explained that he had mistaken Anwen for Nia.

Nia decided to surprise Owen by buying two concert tickets so that she and Owen could go to see her favourite band in the not too distant future. Owen was enthusiastic about the forthcoming concert. Likewise, when the week of the concert arrived, Nia listened to the band's albums and danced around the house singing lyrics from the band's songs.

On the day of the concert, Nia took a day off from work and enjoyed relaxing prior to going to the concert that evening.

She was lying in the bath surrounded by warm water and bubbles when the phone rang.

'Why does the phone always seem to ring when I'm in the bath?' she muttered to herself.

After taking the trouble to get out of the bath, Nia reached the phone just as it stopped ringing. Then she retrieved an answering machine message from Owen saying that he was sorry but something had come up at the last minute and he had to work

She decided that she was going to attend the concert anyway, even if she had to go by herself. Fortunately, despite it being a last minute request, Nia's sister Anwen was more than willing to accompany her for the evening.

By the time that they arrived at the concert, they were feeling quite excited. Queues of people made their way into the concert hall. There was an almost tangible atmosphere of joy and happiness in the hall. Their excitement intensified as the support band began to play. However, they were impatient to see their favourite band on the stage.

Anwen was glad that Nia had made the decision to invite her to go to the concert. The concert was not a disappointment. Anwen and Nia danced to the music and cheered every time the band began to sing another song. Each song was familiar to Nia and Anwen as they had been fans of the band for over a decade.

When the concert was finally over, Nia and Anwen were both in a cheerful mood. They looked at the memorabilia that was on sale at the entrance to the venue before returning to their house.

When they got home, Nia made them both a cup of tea. Despite the enjoyable evening, Nia was disappointed that Owen had let her down.

After their reconciliation, Anwen and Adrian had met up with each other whenever possible. Either Anwen visited Adrian or vice versa. They had been dating for nearly a year when the phone rang and Anwen rushed to answer.

'How are you?' asked Adrian but before Anwen had the chance to reply, he continued, 'I've got good news, would you like to meet me halfway between my house and your house at our favourite hotel to celebrate my news, this weekend?'

'Yes I would love to meet you but I hate suspense, what's your news?' responded Anwen.

'You are cute but I'm afraid that you are going to have to wait,' laughed Adrian. 'Would you like to meet me at the hotel on Saturday at midday?'

'Yes that sounds great,' responded Anwen.

'I'll book for us to stop there.'

'Yes, that would be lovely.'

'It will be my treat,' continued Adrian. 'I look forward to seeing you on Saturday then.'

'I can't wait!' said Anwen.

On the Friday night, Anwen packed an overnight bag in advance for the following night. Nia had pinned a comprehensive ready-made list of what to pack if going on a holiday to the inside of each of their wardrobe doors. Then Anwen had a cup of cocoa and a chat with Nia.

Saturday morning arrived. Anwen had set her alarm for 7 am in the morning. When she woke up, she remembered that she was meeting Adrian and jumped out of bed immediately. It was a cool, fresh morning. The sky was a pale blue. Anwen had a bowl of cereal. Nia was still asleep. At 7.30 am, Anwen made herself a cup of tea and made one for Nia too.

Anwen had a bath then dressed. She wore her deep pink shift dress. She decided to apply some make-up including pale blue eye shadow and pink lipstick.

'How does my make-up look?' asked Anwen.

'It looks nice,' replied Nia.

'Thanks, I just have to get my handbag and my overnight bag and I'll be ready to walk to the train station.'

'I hope you have a lovely time,' said Nia kissing her sister on the cheek. 'I'll see you tomorrow evening and you can tell me how it all went and let me know Adrian's news!'

'Okay,' said Anwen and smiled before giving Nia a hug. 'I'd better go now but I'll see you tomorrow.'

'Bye!' shouted Nia.

Anwen waved to Nia before walking briskly to the train station. She arrived at the train station a few minutes early exactly at the time that she had planned. The train arrived punctually and after climbing onto the train, Anwen found a seat. Fortunately, the train wasn't crowded.

Anwen browsed through a magazine that she had brought with her to look at on the train but she couldn't really concentrate. After looking at it for about twenty minutes, she put the magazine into her overnight bag and looked out of the window.

The train whizzed past views of green trees, patchwork fields and houses. Anwen had to make one train change before she arrived at her destination.

When Anwen arrived at the hotel, Adrian was waiting for her and they gave each other a hug. Adrian gave Anwen a passionate kiss.

'I've missed you!' said Adrian.

'I've missed you too!' responded Anwen. 'And you've kept me in suspense. What's your news?'

'I'm transferring to a dental practice in Wales soon, so we'll be able to see more of one another,' responded Adrian.

'That will be wonderful!' said Anwen happily, 'I'm delighted to hear that, let's have lunch to celebrate!'

They strolled around the town for a while and then found a restaurant that they thought looked like an appealing place to have lunch. After they had sat down in the restaurant and ordered their meal, Adrian leaned across and squeezed Anwen's hand.

'I'm looking forward to us being able to spend more time together,' said Anwen enthusiastically.

When Anwen and Adrian left the restaurant, they walked together hand in hand. Anwen felt content and happy. She was pleased with how well things were progressing between her and Adrian.

Anwen and Adrian meandered around the shops together whilst making their way back to their hotel. Adrian insisted on buying Anwen a rose-coloured nightdress that she happened to remark upon when they passed the shop window in which it had been displayed. Then they returned to their charming hotel.

'I have booked us a room each,' said Adrian. 'I hope that you like your room.'

'Thank you,' replied Anwen. 'Would you like to come to my room for a cup of tea before you unpack?'

'Yes, thanks, that would be great,' responded Adrian.

Anwen filled the small kettle in the room and made two cups of tea. Adrian and Anwen sat on the bed and they sipped their tea and chatted. Then they kissed each other and held one another tightly.

'I wish I hadn't booked two separate rooms for us,' admitted Adrian.

'I wish you hadn't either,' replied Anwen. 'I think one of the rooms that you booked is going to go to waste.'

Chapter 20

After her weekend with Adrian, Anwen caught the train back home on the Sunday afternoon. She was excited to get home because she had a lot of news. Nia greeted her enthusiastically.

'What's the news then?' asked Nia.

'Well Adrian is transferring to a dental practice in Wales soon, so we'll be able to see more of one another,' responded Anwen.

'That's great news!'

'Yes, I can't wait to be able to see more of him.'

'But you'll still be able to see a lot of me too.'

'I know. Things are working out so well.'

'You're lovely and you deserve to be happy!' commented Nia as she gave Anwen a hug.

Because Serena was working away for much of the time, the triplets made the most of opportunities when the three of them had the chance to meet up with each other. Although Anwen and Nia shared a house and saw a lot of each other, they were delighted when Serena confirmed that she would be coming to visit them shortly so that they could celebrate their twenty-sixth birthday together.

The triplets were delighted that on their twenty-sixth birthday, not only did Serena have some time off from her work as a singer on cruise ships, but Nia had a couple of days off from her work as a scientist and Anwen had a couple of days off from her work at the restaurant.

Even though, Serena had moved out of the house that she had been sharing with her sisters, she still kept most of her things in one of the rooms at the house. The triplets liked nothing better than to meet up and go somewhere for a snack and a chat and then go for a browse around the shops and it was even more of a treat if their mother joined them.

On their birthday, the triplets decided that as a treat, the three of them and their mother should pay a visit to a nearby café. They found a table before ordering a mid-afternoon snack. They were soon served a selection of homemade cakes: Welsh cakes; *teisen lap*; and spicy *bara brith* spread with Welsh butter and a pot of tea for four. The Welsh cakes were almost as nice as the ones that their grandmother used to make.

'It's so lovely to see the three of you on your birthday. How is everything going with you all?' asked their mother.

'Well, I'm still enjoying the work on the cruise ships and things are going well with my relationship with Michael, we see each other whenever we get the chance,' said Serena glancing at her engagement ring.

'How is everything going with you Nia?' asked their mother turning her attention to Nia.

'Things are going well,' replied Nia.

'And you Anwen?' enquired their mother.

'Adrian is transferring to a dental practice in Wales shortly, so we'll be able to see more of one another,' responded Anwen.

'That's wonderful news!' exclaimed their mother. 'It sounds as if everything is going well for the three of you, which is great to hear, we often spend our chats trying to solve problems.'

If anyone had a problem, Nia usually gave suggestions for logical solutions, Serena came up with unusual suggestions and Anwen usually tried to think of solutions that would please as many people as possible.

Of the triplets, Serena had the most glamorous career but she refrained from mentioning the times when she missed Anwen, Nia and her mother. Instead, she delighted them with details of the interesting people that she had met, ports that she had visited and local dishes that she had tasted.

'Have you made any plans for the wedding yet?' asked their mother fixing her attention on Serena.

'Yes and I want to make the most of my time off to organize more things in preparation for the wedding, I'm hoping to make some more progress with it today. Nia's been helping me to set up a file to help me organize things,' said Serena.

'It's easy to see what needs to be done because the file is subdivided into different categories such as planning the wedding ceremony, organizing transport, booking a photographer and organizing the catering,' said Nia.

'Plus there's a section in relation to stuff that needs to be done to arrange the honeymoon,' added Serena.

'Well done Nia!' said Anwen. 'And one of my colleagues at the restaurant is a photographer, so I'll give you her number, Serena.'

'That would be great. I've already booked the venue. It's a lovely hotel. And I've chosen the selection of foods to be served at the buffet after the wedding,' announced Serena. 'Chicken and fish dishes will be served and I've taken your advice Anwen and asked them to include a vegetarian selection too.'

'What about guests, who are you inviting?' asked their mother.

'I'm not quite sure yet. I'll invite close family and friends and then decide who else to invite.'

'It's probably a good idea to limit the number of guests or the costs could spiral too much,' suggested Nia.

'But you'd have to make sure that you don't offend certain members of the family by not inviting them if they are expecting an invitation,' offered Anwen.

'Well I must say you sound as if you are making excellent progress with all of the wedding preparations,' said their mother. 'Well done!'

In accordance with Serena's wishes, after finishing their cups of tea, they went to order flowers ready for Serena and Michael's wedding day.

'There's such a lot of choice. All the bouquets look beautiful!' commented their mother as she flicked through the catalogue of floral bouquets.

'I think that a selection of pink flowers would be ideal,' suggested Anwen.

'And the smaller bouquets look perfectly suitable, there's no need to go over the top,' stated Nia.

'I think I'll go for red roses,' concluded Serena and promptly ordered a bridal bouquet of red roses and more red roses, which were to be placed at the wedding venue.

'Excellent choice!' said their mother.

Their next stop was a visit to the local bakery, where the proprietor gave Serena a catalogue of celebration cakes.

The bakery was permeated with the aroma of freshly baked bread. Serena and her sisters and mother all took turns to look at the catalogue.

'Which one do you prefer?' asked their mother.

'I'd suggest fruitcake, it will keep for a long time so it's less likely to go to waste,' suggested Nia.

At the same moment, Anwen said, 'I'd recommend sponge cake, because almost everyone likes plain sponge cake.'

'I'm going to choose chocolate cake,' said Serena.

She placed an order for a three-tiered wedding cake. She also left instructions for it to be decorated with small red hearts and for a little model of a bride and groom to be placed on the top.

'The wedding ceremony is to take place at the same venue as the wedding reception and I've also arranged to have a harpist at the ceremony playing Celtic music,' stated Serena.

'Have you decided where you and Michael will be going for your honeymoon?' asked their mother.

'Yes, we're going to Scotland for a few days!' said Serena.

'That sounds wonderful...' said Anwen.

'Sorry to interrupt but I've just remembered that we have to have one of our routine annual thyroid function blood tests in the next couple of months,' Nia reminded Anwen and Serena.

'I forgot about that, we'll have to arrange them soon,' said Anwen.

'Well, I think the four of us should go to a couple more shops this afternoon and perhaps even help you find a wedding dress Serena!' suggested their mother, changing the subject.

For the rest of the afternoon Nia, Anwen and their mother assisted Serena with the important task of choosing a wedding gown. At the first shop that they visited, Serena didn't see anything that she wanted to buy.

The décor of the second shop was very elegant; deep purple velvet curtains adorned the window and there were crystal chandeliers suspended from the ceiling.

At the second shop, they each picked a dress that they thought Serena should try on.

'Make sure you come out and show us how you look in each dress!' instructed their mother.

'Yes, okay!' Serena smiled and headed for the changing room with the three dresses over her arm.

They waited patiently while Serena went into the changing room to try on each wedding dress. The dress that Nia had chosen for Serena was a very plain white dress with a fitted top and a flared skirt that came to just below the knee.

'It's sensible to have a shorter dress because if it rains, you won't have to worry about the bottom of the dress dragging on the ground,' stated Nia.

Serena tried on Nia's choice first.

'It is nice,' said Serena and she twirled around in the dress, 'but I'm going to have to go for a longer wedding dress.'

Next, Serena tried on Anwen's choice of dress. This time the dress was longer. It had a full skirt, which was covered with a layer of delicate lace.

'Not bad but I think I'd prefer something more fitted,' whispered Serena almost to herself. 'What do you think?'

'Well, you've got to choose the dress that you like the best,' said their mother.

'I'll try on your choice next Mam,' said Serena and walked gracefully back into the changing room, her dress swaying. After a few moments, Serena reappeared from the changing room and asked, 'What do you think?'

She was wearing a long white satin dress, which was fitted down as far as the knees and then flared out below the knees. The bodice was embroidered with sequins. There were satin covered buttons at the back of the dress.

'It's *gorgeous*!' exclaimed Anwen.

'Well at least it only comes down as far as your ankles,' responded Nia, giving a practical viewpoint.

'I think that's the one you have to get, definitely. You look slim and elegant. That dress suits you. You look beautiful!' said their mother.

'Thank you!' responded Serena with a smile and she turned to face herself in the mirror.

Her hair fell around her shoulders and her eyes gleamed with happiness. 'It costs a little bit more than I planned to pay but I love it!'

'And it is a one-off purchase,' commented Anwen.

'Well hopefully it is a one-off purchase,' commented Nia.

'You look like a princess!' exclaimed Anwen and smiled at Serena.

Serena also selected some white satin lingerie. But once, Serena had changed back into her usual clothes, her mother took the dress from her and insisted on buying it for Serena as a gift.

Nia insisted on purchasing a pair of white satin high-heeled shoes for Serena. Then Anwen bought a white wedding veil and a delicate tiara for Serena.

'Thanks! I absolutely love the dress Mam and thank you for the shoes Nia and the veil and tiara Anwen!' said Serena ecstatically.

The wedding dress was carefully placed in the boot of their mother's car. Then, they returned to their parents' house.

'I've really enjoyed myself today,' commented Serena.

'The only problem is that the time's gone too quickly!' concluded Nia.

'Before you walk home, I think it would be appropriate to open a bottle of wine to celebrate your birthday and to celebrate that Serena has made such good progress with her wedding preparations,' announced their mother.

'Good idea!' exclaimed Serena.

'Which wine would you like? Red or white?' asked their mother.

'Let's have some sparkling wine!' suggested Serena.

Their mother called their father to join them and then selected five elegant glasses into which their father poured the effervescent liquid before handing a glass to each of his daughters and his wife and proposing a toast.

'Happy Birthday Anwen, Nia and Serena!' said their father.

'Thanks Dad!' exclaimed Serena then went up to her father and gave him a hug. 'I am really looking forward to the wedding now and looking forward to being married to Michael.'

'Michael is great,' said Anwen.

'I know,' said Serena and beamed.

'We'll be pleased to have Michael as a brother-in-law,' announced Nia.

There was the sound of clinking glasses and then everyone took a sip of sparkling wine. They sat on seats around a centrally placed coffee table. They sipped their wine and chatted to each other. Nia and Anwen missed Serena when she was working away and were enjoying their sister's company.

It was with reluctance that the triplets departed from their parents' house. When they returned to Anwen and Nia's house, Nia began to clear up some dishes that she wished she'd done earlier. Anwen made cups of milky coffee for all three of them.

Serena felt a deep sense of satisfaction at the way in which the day had gone; she'd had a wonderful time. She smiled widely as she rang Michael to update him on all that she'd achieved and to find out how his day had been.

Chapter 21

A few weeks later, Adrian moved to Wales and Anwen spent as much time as possible at Adrian's house. A week later, Adrian announced that he was taking Anwen out for a meal. At the end of the meal as they were eating their fruit and cream, Adrian suddenly stopped eating and looked at Anwen intently.

'What's wrong? Have I got cream on my nose or something?' asked Anwen.

'No but there's something that I want to ask you.'

'What's that then?' enquired Anwen.

'I love you Anwen!' said Adrian as he rose from his chair and got down on one knee. 'Will you marry me?'

'Yes, of course!' responded Anwen immediately and they hugged each other.

Adrian put a dainty gold ring set with diamonds and an amethyst onto Anwen's finger and said, 'Let's get married as soon as possible.'

'Yes, we could organize something simple quite quickly,' agreed Anwen.

'Let's not do anything complicated,' said Adrian. 'We'll just have a simple ceremony at the registry office and invite close family and friends to a nearby hotel for a buffet.'

'I agree,' said Anwen.

Anwen went on a shopping trip with her mother and Adrian's mother and she found a modestly priced pale pink satin dress with a full skirt that reached to just below her knees. On another day, Anwen went shopping with Adrian and they bought their wedding rings ready for their wedding day. A pattern inspired by Celtic artwork adorned each gold ring. Anwen booked the wedding reception at a local hotel. The wedding was due to take place within a matter of weeks.

Serena was pleased but also a little disappointed that Anwen's wedding was scheduled to take place before her own. Nia was impressed that Anwen's arrangements were more economical than Serena's wedding plans.

Close family and friends came to Anwen and Adrian's wedding ceremony and to their wedding reception at a nearby hotel as planned.

After the festivities of their wedding day, Adrian and Anwen said goodbye to their wedding guests.

Anwen and Adrian walked upstairs to their honeymoon suite at the hotel. The suite was adorned with mahogany furniture upholstered in crimson velvet but the centrepiece of the bedroom was a mahogany four-poster bed covered with a deep crimson velvet bedspread and surrounded by matching curtains. On the opposite side of the room, there were matching velvet curtains, which reached to the floor. Anwen parted the curtains to see what lay behind them. She discovered doors, which she opened prior to stepping out onto a small balcony surrounded by wrought-iron railings.

Adrian joined her on the balcony and put his arm around her shoulders. Silver stars filled the night sky and the full moon looked like a beautiful silver lantern.

'This has been a perfect day,' whispered Anwen.

Adrian smiled and leaned over to kiss her hair breathing in the fragrance of lavender.

'Shall we retire for the night?' asked Adrian.

'Yes,' said Anwen and glanced at Adrian.

'You look animated,' said Adrian.

They stepped back into the room and drew the curtains. Adrian placed his suit and shirt over one of the armchairs and slipped beneath the sheets of the four-poster bed. Anwen slipped out of her wedding dress to reveal a pale pink satin bodice, matching pants and white stockings topped with lace but she was still wearing her white satin high-heeled shoes.

'You look slim and shapely,' said Adrian.

'Thank you!' said Anwen. Her gratitude was heartfelt. She had hated it when she had gained weight due to hypothyroidism in childhood because she'd hated the mockery that she'd had to endure. Anwen kicked off her shoes before climbing onto the end of the bed and she crawled towards Adrian who was leaning against a stack of pillows in crisp white pillowcases. Anwen pulled back the bedspread and sheets to reveal Adrian's muscular body.

Anwen began to kiss Adrian lightly. Adrian clasped Anwen's shoulders pulling her towards him and started kissing her passionately on the lips. Anwen loved Adrian's kisses. The day and the night exceeded Anwen's expectations.

One evening, after Anwen and Adrian had got married, they perused a pizza menu and Anwen phoned to order a pizza. In the meantime, they snuggled together on the settee watching a romantic comedy. Adrian knew that Anwen hated any films that contained violence or had a sad ending. When the pizza arrived, Anwen divided it onto two plates.

Adrian poured chilled white wine into two wine glasses. Condensation quickly formed on the outside of the glasses.

'Cheers!' said Adrian as their glasses clinked together.

'*Iechyd da*!' said Anwen contentedly.

'What does that mean?' asked Adrian.

'It means "Good health" in Welsh.'

'I love you,' said Adrian. 'I'm really glad that we're married. However, in the future, I hope that it won't just be the two of us living here, I would like to try for a baby with you at some point.'

'I would too,' said Anwen earnestly.

Chapter 22

Shortly after Anwen and Adrian's wedding, the triplets met up with each other one morning so that they could go for their routine thyroid function blood tests together.

'It's a lovely day. The morning air is so fresh that it reminds me of ice cream,' said Anwen.

'I think I know what you mean,' agreed Serena.

'I don't!' stated Nia.

They went to their local hospital for the blood tests. They would have to wait a couple of weeks before they could go to see their general practitioner to find out the results of their blood tests and get their thyroxine prescriptions refilled.

Serena had a few months at home before her next cruise contract and she was keen to sort out her thyroxine prescriptions out of the way before she returned to work. Although she was away intermittently, she still saw Michael as much as she could and she saw her sisters and parents whenever possible.

Serena and Michael had of course invited their families and friends to their forthcoming wedding. Serena had invited her sisters, her parents, her cousin Carys, friends from university and a few friends that she had made during her work on various cruise ships. Michael had invited his parents and a few friends.

Serena and Michael were paying for half the cost of the wedding each. She did not want to use up all of her savings on the wedding because she was aware that there were other impending costs. The house where Michael lived was more sparsely furnished than she would have liked and they would need to purchase more furniture. Therefore, she took some of Anwen's advice about ways in which she could limit costs.

Serena had enjoyed living in a small house with her sisters and she found it fun to stay in a cabin but she was utterly excited at the thought of living with Michael.

The day of their visit to see their general practitioner arrived. Although, the triplets had made three separate, consecutive appointments with their general practitioner to find out their blood test results, they kept each other company during their separate appointments.

'After looking at your recent blood test results, I am afraid that your thyroxine treatment needs to be decreased with immediate effect; here are your new prescriptions for your reduced daily dose of thyroxine,' said the general practitioner as he peered at the triplets.

'But we feel well!' protested Serena.

'What if we become ill?' asked Nia.

'I am sorry but even if you feel well, the thyroid stimulating hormone test indicates that your dose is too high and therefore your thyroxine dose needs to be lowered for your own good,' said the general practitioner firmly.

'We are happy to stay on our current level of thyroxine,' stated Serena.

'I'm very concerned about the potential adverse consequences if you don't lower your dose in line with your blood test results,' said their general practitioner.

'Okay, I guess we'll have to give it a try,' said Anwen reluctantly.

They walked back to their parents' house in silence. They hadn't had to think about their hypothyroidism since childhood. The possibility that the lowering of their thyroxine dose could lead to a recurrence of the symptoms of hypothyroidism that they had suffered during childhood was disconcerting.

When they entered their parents' kitchen, their father was sitting at the table having a cup of tea with their mother.

'What on earth is wrong?' asked their mother, alarmed at the desolate expressions on their faces.

'We've been told to reduce our daily thyroxine dose, just because of numbers on a piece of paper – not because we're feeling ill or anything like that,' said Serena.

'Why didn't you refuse?' asked their father.

'Well, he's the one who writes the prescriptions and he's concerned that we are taking too much and warned us about potential adverse health effects if we don't lower our dose. It's all quite frightening,' said Serena.

'We are also concerned about potential adverse health effects if we do lower our thyroxine dose but we'll make sure we keep a diary of how we are feeling so that if there are any problems we can go back to the general practitioner and get things sorted straightaway,' said Nia.

'Perhaps it will be okay, they should know what they're talking about, they adjust people's doses all the time,' said Anwen in an attempt to reassure everyone.

Serena hadn't yet told Michael that she had hypothyroidism so when she next met up with Michael, she didn't see any need to tell him that she was about to have her thyroxine dose lowered.

Michael looked intently into Serena's eyes and smiled at her before kissing her and giving her a hug and asking, 'How are you, my darling?'

'I'm fine, thanks. I've been looking forward to meeting up with you again.'

'I've missed you, so I couldn't be better now that you are here with me.'

'That's a sweet thing to say,' said Serena.

'Let's go for something to eat then,' suggested Michael.

'Okay,' said Serena.

They walked to a rustic looking café and found themselves a cosy place to sit in a quiet corner of the café.

Red gingham curtains adorned the Georgian style windows. Red gingham tablecloths covered the round tables.

A red candleholder had been placed on each tablecloth. Each candleholder contained a white candle. They ordered a salad and both had a glass of chilled fruit juice.

'Thanks for all that you've been doing in preparation for the wedding,' said Michael.

'That's all right,' said Serena. 'To be honest I've had lots of help from my sisters, Nia has produced a folder in which all the details can be kept organized and Anwen helped me to write all of the invitations.'

'That's good of them,' responded Michael as he grasped hold of Serena's hand and squeezed her hand affectionately. 'I've got a present for you as a little token of my appreciation.'

'Thank you,' said Serena as he passed her a small pink velvet box. She leant over and gave Michael a kiss before opening the box, inside of which was a locket. Serena opened the locket to see a photo of her on one side of the locket and a photo of Michael on the other side.

'I love you,' said Michael and held Serena's hand. 'I'm so happy that we've found each other and am looking forward to us being together.'

'I love you too and the locket is beautiful, thank you.'

'How is everything going with work?' asked Michael.

'I'm enjoying it but as we planned, I'll hand in my notice before the wedding so that I can look for work locally once we're married,' said Serena enthusiastically.

'Yes, I have local work lined up for myself already. I can't wait to be able to see more of you!'

'I know. I feel the same!'

'I want to be able to wake up each morning and see your lovely face and then cuddle you and have breakfast with you,' said Michael.

'I can't wait! We can spend time together in the day even if we'll often be working at different venues in the evenings.'

'Now, let's go back to my house and we could watch a film together if you like,' said Michael looking intently at Serena as he smiled and squeezed her hand again.

'Okay, that sounds great to me, can't wait!' said Serena knowing that they would be spending more time kissing and cuddling each other than watching the film.

They wanted to make the most of one another's company because Michael was about to start a six month contract on a cruise ship and Serena had a couple of months in South Wales before she would be commencing a six month contract on a different cruise ship.

Chapter 23

Unfortunately, after only a short time on the lower thyroxine dose, all three of the triplets started to develop symptoms of under-treated hypothyroidism.

One weekend, Nia decided to have a walk around the shops. As she walked along the pavements, she was aware that she felt a little out of breath, despite the fact that she usually walked regularly without experiencing any problems. Anwen felt breathless when walking upstairs at the restaurant. Serena noticed feeling breathless too.

Nia had also noticed that the skin on her scalp had thickened. This reminded her of being hypothyroid in childhood. She decided that she'd have to make a note of this in her diary. Anwen and Serena noticed the same thing.

Shortly after that, the triplets started to notice sharp pains in their forearms, wrists and hands: simple movements were painful such as holding a piece of toast, holding cutlery or holding a cup.

At work in the laboratory, Nia noticed that preparing samples for analysis was giving her sharp, painful twinges in her wrists.

This prompted a visit to their general practitioner but they were told that they had to be patient until they adjusted to the reduced thyroxine dose.

The triplets never usually had any problems fitting into their clothes. However, after a relatively short time on the reduced thyroxine dose, they commented to each other that they were having difficulty zipping up some of their dresses.

This was despite the fact that they were sensible about what they ate most of the time and the fact that they had observed that their appetite had decreased following the reduction in their thyroxine dose.

After being mocked for the weight gain that had resulted from hypothyroidism during childhood, they felt disconcerted at the knowledge that they were gaining weight.

During the lunch break, Nia would sometimes stroll to the nearby shop, buy some sandwiches and then walk back to work. She knew that this walk always took her half an hour so she never needed to look at her watch but it suddenly started to take her around twice as long and she was horrified when she arrived back at work and looked at her watch and realized that she was late.

Colleagues commented that Nia and Anwen were wearing cardigans when everyone else was wearing thin blouses or shirts. Serena noted that she felt cold all the time too.

Anwen would spend the day at the restaurant then she would go home to the house that she had recently moved to with Adrian and practically go straight to bed.

A little more time elapsed and the triplets noticed that the slightest exertion was giving them chest pains. They had always enjoyed walking but they started to have twinges of pain in their chests after walking only very short distances. They had always exercised regularly to keep fit and for fun but they began to find that after only a couple of minutes of exercise, they would also experience twinges of pain in their chest.

Their general practitioner told them to be patient and reassured them that they would adjust to the lowered thyroxine dose in due course.

Serena wasn't able to return to the cruise ship and fulfil her contract and remained at the house that she had previously shared with her sisters.

The triplets' symptoms increased in severity and frequency. They felt their energy slipping away. Before long, Nia wasn't up to going into the laboratory and Anwen wasn't well enough to go to the restaurant.

Superimposed upon the breathlessness, chest pains, and wrist, hand and forearm pains was the insidious yet unrelenting surge in the levels of exhaustion that the triplets were experiencing. They noticed that they felt exhausted all the time and were sleeping for longer at night.

Again, their general practitioner informed them that adjustment to their lowered thyroxine dose would require a little more time.

Adrian was concerned about leaving Anwen alone in their house. Therefore, he would give her a lift to her sisters' house before he started work each day so that she could spend the day with them.

Owen had been exhibiting his art at a gallery in Paris for a few months. However, when he returned, the difference in the appearance of Anwen, Nia and Serena gave him a jolt.

Nia looked pale and sallow. Her lips were devoid of their usual crimson hue and her face looked puffy. Her movements were slow in comparison to usual. However, Owen continued to visit Nia regularly.

In addition, neither Serena nor Anwen looked their usual selves. Their cheeks were no longer rosy in appearance, their lips were pale in colour and their hands were cold.

'How are you feeling?' asked their mother when she visited the triplets one day.

'I'm feeling terrible, something is not right,' said Anwen.

'I dreamt that I'd spilt anaesthetic on my hands and that I was desperately trying to wash it off because they'd gone numb and when I woke up my hands had gone numb,' said Nia.

'Sometimes, I wake up screaming because of the pain in my hands and wrists,' commented Serena.

Their mother glanced at her daughters with a look of concern on her face. The triplets were horrified that they had gone into such a sharp decline but at the same time, the dose reduction had made them exhausted and stupefied. However, paradoxically, though the horror at their own situation was muted by exhaustion, even the exhaustion that overwhelmed them couldn't prevent them from feeling deep concern at the sight of the decline in one another.

'This is scary, we shouldn't be feeling like this, this shouldn't be happening, we'll have to go and see the doctor again about this,' stated Nia.

Chapter 24

'We'll have to see the doctor again as soon as possible so I'm going to book the appointments now,' said Anwen firmly.

Appointments were duly obtained and the triplets went to see their general practitioner. The triplets were satisfied that they had spent enough time on the lower thyroxine dose to demonstrate that it was insufficient for their individual needs.

'I'm afraid that the decrease in our thyroxine dose isn't suiting us,' said Nia.

'Unfortunately, it seems that your body still needs to adjust to the lower thyroxine dose so you do need to be patient,' said the general practitioner.

'But what about the terrible pains in our wrists that we've all been experiencing?' queried Nia.

'It sounds like the three of you may have developed carpal tunnel syndrome,' said the general practitioner.

'What about the exhaustion?' asked Anwen.

'Lots of people find that they are exhausted, I recommend that you take a look at your lifestyle and cut back on your activities.'

'But we are too exhausted to be active and we all feel that we need our thyroxine dose increased urgently!' exclaimed Serena.

'I'm going to refer the three of you to an orthopaedic surgeon immediately in relation to the problems that you are experiencing with your hands. As for your thyroxine dose, I suggest that you stay on the lower dose to give yourselves more time to adjust to it,' said the general practitioner firmly.

The triplets left the general practitioner's office and looked at one another in despair. Anwen felt tears welling up in her eyes.

'This is a nightmare, it would be useful to know how long we are going to take to adjust to our lower thyroxine dose,' said Nia.

'Since I've started taking a lower dose of thyroxine, it's had a very bad effect on me but I want to be better before my wedding,' added Serena.

'I feel exhausted *despite* being inactive so I'm unable to sustain my usual lifestyle,' stated Anwen.

'I feel as if I'm not my usual self and as if I'm thinking less,' admitted Nia.

'I feel as if I'm talking less,' said Serena.

'And everything is a ridiculous effort,' added Anwen.

Their mother took the triplets back to her house after their appointment then their mother made a cup of tea for them and they discussed their situation further. She was deeply concerned about the impact that the lowering of their thyroxine dose was having on the triplets. She remembered the problems that they'd experienced in childhood.

'Sometimes, my lungs feel as if I'm not getting enough air,' said Serena.

'The overwhelming exhaustion makes me feel how I'd imagine someone would feel if they'd been given strong sedatives,' stated Nia.

'Yes, I feel as if I'm doing well if I come downstairs and lie on the settee rather than on the bed,' commented Anwen.

'Our expectations have fallen pitifully low!' exclaimed Nia.

'Carpal tunnel syndrome restricts our hands and wrists like an invisible rope,' lamented Anwen.

'Yes, it does,' said Nia.

'The unrelenting exhaustion isn't diminished by rest and sleep; it's like an invisible captor,' declared Serena.

'True, and yet even though we know how bad things are and we're aware of how awful we feel, a stranger looking at us wouldn't realize how much we'd declined and they wouldn't realize how much our capabilities have decreased,' added Nia.

'Yes, the condition is overwhelming and yet simultaneously insidious,' concluded Anwen.

'It's so difficult to convey how we are feeling because the pain is invisible!' exclaimed Serena.

'I'm concerned in case we don't adjust to this lower thyroxine dose,' admitted Nia with a serious expression on her face.

On another occasion, at the house that she shared with Adrian, Anwen lay on the bed staring at the ceiling, she felt exhausted but the pains in her hands, wrists and forearms prevented her from sleeping. Adrian had been reading downstairs but he put his book away, came upstairs and bounced onto the bed next to her.

'I haven't got the energy to bounce onto the bed anymore,' muttered Anwen.

'Let's cuddle,' said Adrian.

'Okay,' said Anwen and they both turned to lie on their side facing one another and Anwen made a feeble attempt to caress his shoulder.

'Stop!' he said. 'Your hands are freezing. Let me warm them up.'

'I don't think I can continue caressing you anyway,' said Anwen dolefully, 'because my hands are hurting too much.'

'Your feet are freezing too!' exclaimed Adrian. 'Never mind, I'll caress you instead.' Adrian unbuttoned her pyjama top. He slid his hand under her top and caressed Anwen. 'You never wear your rose-coloured nightdress anymore,' commented Adrian.

'I've put on so much weight since having my daily thyroxine dose reduced that it probably wouldn't even fit me any longer and even if I did manage to fit into it, it would probably split at the seams,' complained Anwen.

'Don't worry. You still look attractive to me. I'd like to make love to you right now,' said Adrian.

'I'm sorry, I do love you. However, I haven't got the energy to even think about that.'

'That's okay, I understand,' said Adrian as he removed his hand from Anwen and lay on his back again.

A little while later, Anwen did fall asleep.

'Stop snoring!' said Adrian as he nudged her gently so that she woke up. 'You didn't snore before you developed the symptoms of hypothyroidism. I think it's another symptom.'

'I wasn't snoring!' said Anwen half sleepily and half defensively.

Anwen fell asleep again and began to snore again. Adrian decided that it would be unfair to wake her a second time and switched off his bedside lamp.

'Trying for a baby is out of the question until you are well again,' muttered Adrian to himself.

More time elapsed. The triplets made intermittent phone calls to their general practitioner. However, they were advised to continue to be patient whilst their body adjusted to the lower thyroxine dose. They didn't seem to be adjusting to their lower dose of thyroxine. Their parents tried to provide the triplets with as much help as possible and took them to see the hospital phlebotomist for further thyroid function blood tests. They waited in suspense for their blood test results in the hope that the results would convince their general practitioner to raise their thyroxine dose back to its original level so that they would stop suffering from the symptoms of under-treated hypothyroidism.

Their health deteriorated further and the slightest exertion would need to be followed by hours of rest or sleep However, they were informed that their thyroid stimulating hormone levels were within the reference range and that they needed to allow even more time to adjust to the lower thyroxine dose.

When Michael contacted Serena whilst he was working on the cruise ship, she felt that she had no choice but to confide in him about her hypothyroidism and the bad effect that the lowering of her thyroxine dose was having on her while she waited to adjust to the lower dose. He seemed sympathetic. When he next returned home, he came to visit Serena whenever he had the opportunity. One day he found her flopped onto the settee. She had a fleece throw draped around her shoulders. She felt too exhausted to move.

'Why have you switched the heating on?' asked Michael.

'It's cold,' explained Serena. 'Feel my hands, they are freezing cold.'

'What have you been doing?'

'I've been sleeping throughout the day!' said Serena as tears started to spill from her eyes. The tears gave way to loud sobs and between the sobs she tried to express how she was feeling, 'I can't stand this. I've just gone downhill since my thyroxine dose was lowered and I'll be trapped like this if I can't get my treatment increased again.'

'You are reliant on the doctors because they are the ones who prescribe your thyroxine for you,' said Michael, 'but perhaps things wouldn't be so bad if you tried to push yourself to do more.'

The frustration of feeling so unwell and the difficulty in getting Michael to understand and in getting the medical profession to understand suddenly overwhelmed Serena and she continued to sob in despair.

He looked alarmed and rushed across the room, knelt beside the settee and put his arms on her shoulders.

'Be quiet or the neighbours will be wondering what's going on!' he urged.

'I'm sorry for getting so upset, it's just that I feel like I've aged overnight,' explained Serena. 'I know that every time you've wanted to cuddle me lately, I've just wanted to go to sleep but that's because of the effect that the reduction in the thyroxine dose has been having on me. If I'm not myself lately, it's not because I'm losing interest in you!'

'You'll have to go back to the doctor as soon as possible, I'm sure everything can be sorted out.'

However, after another visit to their doctor and more blood tests, the results of the triplets' blood tests still indicated that they were on the correct thyroxine dose and they were informed that no increase in their thyroxine dose could be justified but that other causes of their symptoms would be investigated.

On another occasion, the triplets had been given separate appointments with different general practitioners. Serena was told that she might be starting to suffer from anxiety, Nia was advised that she was probably experiencing a certain amount of depression and Anwen was told that she could be starting to develop chronic fatigue syndrome or fibromyalgia.

Chapter 25

Things worsened when a little while later, the triplets started to have nausea, dizziness and balance problems. They would be struck by the balance problems without warning causing them to fall flat on the floor.

When they were at home, if they needed to cross the room, they would walk slowly and carefully around the room with their hands on the wall or furniture but their faulty balance still caused them to fall flat on the floor or against the furniture on numerous occasions.

This symptom was particularly disturbing because it was both unpleasant and dangerous. Anwen fell backwards in the kitchen confirming to the triplets that it would be too dangerous for them to attempt to use an oven.

The other disturbing thing about this new symptom was that it was dangerous for them to go out on their own, as they were liable to fall and thus they could be a risk to themselves.

'I've never had sea sickness whilst working on cruise ships and now here on dry land, I'm feeling nauseous nearly all the time and I have difficulty crossing the living room,' said Serena dolefully.

After another visit to their doctor to report the dizziness, their doctor was still unwilling to contemplate providing the triplets with prescriptions for their original dose of thyroxine but said, 'I can prescribe some medication to ease the nausea and I can refer you all to the local ear, nose and throat specialist.'

'But what about our thyroxine dose, will you increase it?' asked the triplets simultaneously.

'The lowering of the thyroxine dose must have caused the balance problems,' said Nia who valued scientific detachment and logic.

'I've not heard of a decrease in someone's thyroxine dose leading to balance problems,' said the general practitioner. 'Have further blood tests and get in touch for your results in the next fortnight.'

The triplets had been on the lowered dose for a while and were worried that unless their blood test results altered to correlate with their symptoms of hypothyroidism, they would be dismissed as hypochondriacs. Their mother had to take them to the outpatient department of the local hospital for the dreaded blood tests.

During the tests, Nia would force herself to watch but Anwen and Serena would stare in the opposite direction.

The phlebotomist was excellent and the blood tests weren't as bad as they expected and were soon over and they left the hospital with their mother.

'Oh dear, what's going to become of you three?' asked their mother.

'This is a very frightening experience and we are all worried about each other but let's hope that these thyroid function tests including the thyroid stimulating hormone test will confirm that we have indeed become hypothyroid so that the doctors will be willing to increase our dose again,' said Anwen.

'Yes, I hope that our blood test results correlate with our symptoms so that we can have our thyroxine dose increased,' stated Serena.

The triplets were eager to contact their general practitioner to find out the results of their most recent blood tests.

'Hi, I'm phoning to see if my blood test result has come in,' said Nia.

Their cousin Carys worked on reception at their general practitioners' practice but another member of staff answered the phone.

'Please may I have your name and date of birth?' asked the receptionist.

Nia supplied the information requested and waited tensely while the receptionist pulled up her file on the computer screen.

'Your thyroid function tests are normal, your thyroxine dose is correct,' said the receptionist.

'That can't be right!' exclaimed Nia.

'If you want to discuss the blood test results, you'll have to make an appointment with the general practitioner.'

'I'll phone back later,' said Nia and put the phone down then looked at Anwen and Serena glumly.

Anwen and Serena phoned in turn next, only to discover that despite their severe symptoms of hypothyroidism, their thyroid function test results were in the reference range too. The day of their appointment with the general practitioner arrived. They arranged their three appointments in sequence with the same doctor and kept one another company.

'This situation is dire, perhaps there is usually a correlation between symptoms of hypothyroidism and thyroid function test results but unfortunately *in our case*, there doesn't seem to be the expected correlation between our symptoms and our blood test results,' said Nia to the general practitioner.

'The thyroid function tests are very sensitive and indicate that the lower dose is the correct dose for the three of you,' said the general practitioner.

'Please could we be referred to an endocrinologist?' begged Anwen.

'Certainly,' said the general practitioner.

After their appointment, the triplets' mother took them back to the house that Serena and Nia shared.

'It is a nightmare to feel so ill due to the symptoms of hypothyroidism!' exclaimed Serena.

131

'Not only that, I'm really worried about our financial situation now, we've ended up using up most of our savings,' said Nia.

'I hope that we'll be able to recover soon and return to work and start earning a wage again, I'm worried about the future,' said Anwen and tears started to trickle down her face.

'Here's a hanky, Anwen,' said Serena as she passed Anwen a handkerchief.

'When we are well again, we'll have to make it known that in our case, sole reliance on the thyroid function test results led to problems,' vowed Nia.

'We'll have to make the point that our illness due to an incorrectly low dose of thyroxine is not anyone's fault but because *in our case*, our thyroid stimulating hormone levels haven't risen as expected in response to insufficient thyroxine,' stated Anwen.

'Yes, it is really difficult for us to convey the message that our thyroxine dose is too low when our thyroid stimulating hormone levels are being interpreted to mean that our thyroxine dose is correct,' added Nia.

'Yes and the symptoms of hypothyroidism are the opposite of glamorous and they don't seem to evoke much sympathy,' muttered Serena.

'You feel as if your symptoms are dismissed. Just get more sleep if you are tired! It's not that simple!' said Nia bitterly.

'Or just eat less if you weigh more!' added Serena.

'Or if you're having too many symptoms, you must just be a hypochondriac,' chimed Nia.

'Hypothyroidism makes you feel so useless,' said Anwen desolately. 'Hypothyroidism steals your mental and physical energy and makes you feel useless to society.'

'I agree,' said Serena.

The triplets were invited to attend numerous appointments, including ones with an orthopaedic surgeon who said that they did have carpal tunnel syndrome and informed them that as a result, they needed to be put on the waiting list for surgery.

Then they saw the ear, nose and throat specialist who stated that their balance problems were not caused by hypothyroidism and that they might improve with time.

Despite previously having their hopes for resolutions to their health problems dashed on more than one occasion, the triplets waited in the hope that their forthcoming appointments with the endocrinologist would lead to them being prescribed their original dose of thyroxine again and being able to recover from their symptoms of under-treated hypothyroidism.

Nia couldn't help starting to panic about their health problems and their inability to work but also prided herself on being pragmatic and tried to put on a brave face as much as possible.

Although Anwen was struggling to do the simplest things due to her symptoms of under-treated hypothyroidism, she tried to reassure herself and her sisters that all of their health problems would soon be resolved once they had consulted the endocrinologist.

Serena on the other hand voiced her doubts that she and Nia would be able to remain living in their house together for much longer despite the fact that their parents were providing them with help and support.

'Unless we can find a doctor who'll help us, I think that we are in grave danger,' warned Serena before widening her eyes and shuddering.

The triplets didn't have the energy to do housework and members of their family would take it in turns to carry out household tasks for Nia and Serena.

Adrian had taken over all household tasks on behalf of Anwen because he knew that she wasn't well enough to do housework.

To the triplets' dismay, they could no longer fit into some of their clothes. Serena's penchant for fitted dresses meant that she had been affected first and needed to borrow some of Nia and Anwen's looser fitting clothes. Nia had been affected next. She could no longer squeeze into her jeans and asked to borrow some of Anwen's clothes too.

Their mother had to step in and provide more help for them. It was too difficult for them to get ready without help. They waited for a visit from their mother before they attempted to bath because not only did bathing require an overwhelming amount of energy, their balance problems meant that they were fearful of getting out of the bath unsupervised in case they fell over. Even Anwen became reliant upon getting ready at her sisters' house under the supervision of their mother.

One day when their mother was helping Anwen and Nia to get ready, Serena put her arms in the sleeves of her woollen dress and pulled the dress over her head but before she could pull the dress down onto herself, her balance problems caused her to fall flat onto the floor with a loud thud.

'Are you okay?' asked her mother anxiously.

'Yes, I'm okay. Thankfully!' replied Serena. 'Who would have thought that even getting dressed would become a dangerous activity?'

Their mother would also take one of the triplets with her to get groceries each week. The triplet allocated to go shopping would hold onto their mother so that if they started to fall, they could grab onto their mother for support.

Prior to the reduction in their thyroxine dose, the triplets' lives had been a hectic mix of work and social arrangements with family and friends.

Now, they muddled through the days, their energy levels were low, their need for rest and sleep was high but their pain levels were also high and this disrupted their sleep. Each day dragged. They experienced an alternating mosaic of exhaustion, pain and balance problems that rendered them useless in all areas of their lives.

Chapter 26

By the time that the triplets saw the endocrinologist, they had been on the lower thyroxine dose for nearly a year. They decided that rather than trying to explain everything and risk forgetting something important, they'd write everything down. They held onto one another for support as they went into the endocrinologist's office. The endocrinologist was handsome and clean-shaven and was surrounded by the aroma of lemon aftershave. They handed him a carefully prepared explanation of their situation. He read the piece of paper nodding to himself as he did and Serena, Nia and Anwen felt a mixture of nervousness and excitement at the possibility that they were about to receive help at last.

He raised his head and looked at the three sisters, 'I am sorry but the thyroid function test results indicate that you are on the correct dose of thyroxine and therefore any symptoms that you are experiencing are not due to hypothyroidism.'

The triplets looked at one another and widened their eyes.

'I'm sorry, there isn't anything further that I can do,' said the endocrinologist apologetically as he handed the piece of paper back to them.

The appointment ended. The triplets felt dismayed and abandoned. Their parents took them home. They weren't up to doing anything apart from spending the day resting. Attempts to do more than that proved too difficult.

The triplets knew that they were suffering from severe symptoms of hypothyroidism but because *in their case*, their blood test results didn't happen to correlate with their symptoms, they couldn't get any medical professionals to increase their prescribed dose of thyroxine back to its original level.

Even if most hypothyroid patients' blood test results correlated with their symptoms, Serena, Anwen and Nia's blood test results did not correlate with their symptoms and the consequences of this were terrifying.

Their mother helped them to write letters in which they explained their situation and asked their general practitioner and endocrinologist for help but each letter eventually prompted a dismissive reply.

Serena was particularly desperate because she was due to get married soon. When her mother took her for the final fitting of her wedding dress, she couldn't even pull the dress up over her hips. Serena sobbed in despair and had to order a completely different style of wedding dress at the last moment.

The wedding day of Serena and Michael arrived. Serena reached over and switched off her alarm clock.

'My wedding,' Serena whispered, 'I'm too exhausted for my own wedding.'

The telephone rang and Serena reached over to answer the phone.

'How are you today? No second thoughts?' asked the familiar voice of her cousin Carys.

'No, none at all,' said Serena. 'But I wish I wasn't feeling so ill.'

'You'll be okay, look forward to seeing you later,' said Carys.

Serena liked the house that she shared with Nia but her parents had packed up most of her possessions ready for transportation to the house that she would be sharing with Michael once they were married.

Serena's mother came to help Serena to get ready for her wedding. After a bath, Serena got dressed in the larger sized white satin dress. She had met the man of her dreams. She was completely and utterly in love with him. However, she wished that she wasn't ill.

She would be moving in with Michael shortly but feared that she would be unable to meet his expectations. She tried to phone Michael for a quick chat before the wedding ceremony. Since he had returned to Wales to live, they usually contacted each other at least once a day on days when they weren't seeing each other. However, she couldn't get an answer. He usually answered the phone immediately but he was probably in a rush to get ready himself.

Adrian had also dropped Anwen off at Nia and Serena's house so that she could see Serena prior to the wedding. Anwen and Nia knocked Serena's bedroom door and came into her room just as Serena was standing in front of a long mirror looking at her reflection. Their mother tried to fasten a couple of buttons that were awkward for Serena to reach at the back of her wedding dress but to no avail. Serena had filled out since ordering the newer dress and it was just not possible to do up the buttons. Therefore, Anwen lent Serena her silver shrug to wear to disguise this fact. Anwen attempted to fasten a pearl necklace that she was lending Serena for the day around Serena's neck but the pain in her fingers prevented her from doing so and she had to ask their mother for help with the task.

Serena kissed Anwen and Nia before they left the house and told them that it would not be long before the wedding limousine came to collect her and her mother. Nia and Anwen were then picked up by Owen and Adrian respectively.

Serena felt concerned that she was still suffering from the symptoms of under-treated hypothyroidism and worried that she would be a burden to Michael.

She had already packed for her honeymoon in Scotland but they would not be leaving until the day after the wedding. She was hoping that she could have a restful honeymoon. She didn't have the energy for more than rest.

Serena heard the sound of a car outside and looked out of the window to see if the limousine had arrived even though it was not due yet.

She recognized the car outside as belonging to Michael. As she walked carefully downstairs, she heard the sound of his car door slam shut, followed by the clank of her letterbox, followed by the sound of his car door slamming once more. She glanced out of the window to see his car accelerating away.

She walked over to the door to see what had been put through her letterbox. She was carrying her white satin bag and the bridal bouquet of red roses so she put them on the table and picked up a white envelope that had fallen onto the doormat.

Serena read her name on the outside of the envelope. She tore open the envelope and started to read its contents:

Dear Serena,

Thank you for all the wonderful times that we have spent together. I am sorry to have to tell you today but I have been thinking about everything and I no longer think that it is a good idea for us to get married today. Please forgive me for the timing of my message and accept my apologies. I wish you all the best.

Take care of yourself.
Michael

Serena could not believe her eyes. She had been expecting a cheerful message from Michael to say that he was looking forward to seeing her or a romantic message.

Why had Michael not given her any indication leading up to this day that he was having second thoughts about their relationship? Was there something wrong with her intuition? She had thought that her relationship with Michael was good.

This was very bad news, not only that but she would have to let everyone know that the wedding was off. On the previous day, she had been praising Michael. Serena rubbed her forehead. She tried to compose herself before going upstairs to tell her mother about the letter. Her mother hugged her then told her that her limousine had arrived. Serena and her mother instructed the driver of the limousine to take them to the hotel that had been booked for both the wedding ceremony and the reception, so that they could inform the staff and wedding guests about the change of plan. The driver did as instructed and Serena thanked him.

'Shall I wait for you here?' asked the driver.

'That won't be necessary thanks,' responded Serena.

She held onto her mother as they walked towards the hotel's entrance. She wobbled slightly due to her balance problems and worried that people would think that she was drunk. She was grateful that her mother was with her.

She had to try to analyse the situation. Perhaps Michael did still want to be with her but he didn't want to go through a wedding ceremony. She felt a glimmer of hope at that thought but then dismissed the thought and burst into tears. She still had to inform all of the guests that there was to be no wedding ceremony.

She decided against seeing everyone and she asked her mother to get the key for the hotel room that she had booked for that night from the receptionist. Her mother took Serena to the room and told her to have a lie down for a while.

'I'll go and let the staff, your father, your sisters and the other guests know what has happened and then I'll come back and put the kettle on, I won't be long,' said her mother.

Whilst waiting for her mother to return, Serena kicked off her white satin heels. She proceeded to pour herself a glass of water and took a few gulps before lying on the bed and staring up at the chandelier on the ceiling. As she lay on the hotel room bed, tears trickled from her eyes. She felt devastated and humiliated that her relationship with Michael had ended this way.

She thought about all of the lovely things that Michael had said to her whilst they had been together but such thoughts made her feel even more upset.

When her mother returned to the hotel room, her mother picked up the little kettle in the room and filled it with water, switched it on to boil and made two cups of tea. She handed one cup of tea on a saucer to Serena.

'Thanks Mam.'

'Don't worry about anything. I've informed everyone that the wedding had to be cancelled.'

'Everyone?'

'I've let the staff here know and I've spoken to your father, your sisters and the other guests.'

'Thanks, I couldn't face doing it myself,' replied Serena glumly then she gave her mother a hug and began sobbing as she thought back to the last time that she had met up with Michael.

Chapter 27

Later that day, Serena's mother took Serena back to the house that she was now going to be continuing to share with her sister Nia. Serena was practically inconsolable. She had tried to ring Michael but there had been no reply. Anwen, Nia and their mother tried to comfort Serena.

'Part of my difficulty is that I feel the need for a full explanation from Michael for everything that has happened or rather not happened. If he jilted me because of the hypothyroidism, I need him to tell me to my face,' replied Serena when asked how she was feeling by their mother.

'That's understandable,' their mother commented.

'Yes, it would be easier if you could speak to him in person,' said Nia in a sympathetic tone of voice.

'Perhaps he just needs some space, perhaps he will be in touch soon,' said Anwen but she suspected that she was not being in the least successful in her attempts to console Serena.

It had turned into a dull, rainy day but Serena didn't care about the gloomy weather. In fact, she was glad about it because somehow the weather matched her miserable mood.

'I am now insecure about my judgement,' stated Serena.

'There's nothing wrong with your judgement,' commented Anwen.

'Well, if I could be so secure about our relationship prior to everything that's happened, what does that say about the accuracy of my intuition and judgement?' argued Serena. 'I just can't tell what someone is thinking and I thought I could but obviously I can't. I feel so stupid that this has happened.'

'But you weren't stupid, he gave you that locket, he wouldn't have done that if he hadn't felt strongly about you when he gave it to you,' said Anwen.

Serena went into her bedroom to retrieve the locket from her jewel box and then opened it and stared at the miniature photo of Michael. After staring at the locket, Serena glanced up at her sisters, her eyes glistening.

'It might be best if you don't keep that locket if it makes you feel upset when you look at it, perhaps you could sell it and buy something different for yourself,' suggested Nia pragmatically.

'I want to keep it,' declared Serena holding it to her chest.

'Perhaps something happened suddenly that you don't know about that caused Michael to change his mind about getting married,' suggested Nia.

'But what could possibly have happened to make him change his mind like that?' asked Serena. 'We've been in touch with each other every day lately; it must be because of the hypothyroidism.'

'Well, I'm sure you will find out what caused him to change his mind at such short notice at some point,' said Anwen as she gave Serena a hug.

'I hate him for doing this to me, I am so annoyed with him,' said Serena. 'Why didn't he have the courage to tell me in person and why didn't he give me a proper reason?' Serena asked.

The unanswered questions whirled around her head.

'I want him back, I love him,' muttered Serena contradicting her previous comment as tears trickled down her cheeks.

'Try to look after yourself and try not to think too far ahead at the moment,' said their mother.

'Everyone is different, I guess,' said Nia. 'That was his way of dealing with some sort of internal conflict.'

Their mother handed Serena a cup of tea, which she sipped slowly.

'Our cousin Carys has tried ringing you a couple of times,' said Nia, 'but you were in bed so I asked her if she could ring back at another time.'

The next day, Serena did think that it might be a good idea to try to instigate some sort of response from Michael by sending a short note to him so that's what she did.

She said how sorry she was that they had not got married. She said how grateful she'd be if he could at least let her know if he did want to continue with their relationship even if he had changed his mind about getting married.

If he didn't want any sort of relationship to be ongoing between them, she asked him if he could at least provide her with an explanation for his change of heart. Serena asked her mother to post the note to him.

The following day, Serena tried ringing Michael's parents who said that he had told them to let her know that he was staying with a friend for a while if she rang but they didn't seem to know when he'd be back.

Serena was grateful for the moral support that she received from her sisters and parents, although Nia voiced her disapproval at Serena's tendency to listen to songs that she had previously listened to with Michael.

On the triplets' twenty-seventh birthday, Owen wanted to spend the day with Nia, and Adrian had taken the day off work to be with Anwen. The triplets' parents called to see Serena during the afternoon. They gave her a birthday card and birthday present.

During her parents' visit, the phone rang. Serena hoped that it would be a phone call from Michael telling her how much he'd missed her and picked up the receiver.

'Hello,' said Serena.

'Hello,' said a female voice. 'Is that Serena, Anwen or Nia?'

'Hi, it's Serena. Is that Carys?'

'Yes, I wanted to wish you a happy birthday and I wanted to find out how you are.'

'I'm all right thanks, well as all right as can be expected. How are you?'

'I'm okay thanks. I could call around if you like but don't worry if it's not convenient.'

'No that's fine, call in,' said Serena glumly.

'I'll be there in one hour. See you soon.'

Serena put down the receiver, turned to her parents and looked despondent.

'What's wrong?' asked her mother anxiously.

'That was Carys. She's calling over in an hour. I want to put everything tidy but I am not up to it. I haven't got the energy to do it,' said Serena.

Serena's parents looked at one another.

'Don't worry, we'll tidy things up for you before Carys comes,' said her mother.

'I wish that I felt up to tidying all this mail away, putting the clothes into the washing machine and doing the dishes,' stated Serena.

'I'll do that,' said her mother and father simultaneously.

'Thanks both, I am grateful!' responded Serena and had a feeling of déjà vu.

Her parents put the living room tidy, did the dishes and put some washing into the washing machine.

'Thanks,' said Serena. 'I'm so grateful but I do feel terrible that I'm relying on you so much.'

'Don't worry about that,' said her mother.

An hour later, the house was looking a bit better. Then, Carys knocked Serena's door.

'It's lovely to see you!' said Serena, relieved that her parents had helpfully put a semblance of order in the living room and kitchen.

'Yes, and you too, I have been thinking about you especially after everything that's happened, how are you?'

'I'm okay, thanks,' said Serena, 'but I feel very let down, the hypothyroidism is a nightmare and I think that's why Michael doesn't want to be with me but it's not my fault, *I've* done nothing wrong…'

'Would you like a cup of tea?' asked Serena's mother.

'Yes please,' said Carys.

'I'm still in emotional turmoil after being jilted by Michael and I can't embark upon the next stage of my life until I can find a doctor who is willing to treat my hypothyroidism properly and make me well again. I feel abandoned by the doctors, abandoned by Michael, I don't know where to turn,' continued Serena.

'I understand,' replied Carys.

'I've still got to return wedding gifts most of which are unopened, my mother has been helping me with that task,' continued Serena.

'That's good of your mother.'

'Part of me still wishes Michael would get in touch and tell me what a stupid mistake he has made and ask me how he can possibly make it up to me so that we can be together!'

'He doesn't deserve someone as lovely as you,' said Carys.

'That's a sweet thing to say,' said Serena, wiping a tear away. 'I shouldn't be crying on my birthday.'

'Let me give you a hug,' said Carys and proceeded to put her arms around Serena.

'Thanks,' said Serena.

'I've got some gifts for you and your sisters for your birthday,' said Carys.

'Thank you,' said Serena.

'I'll put your gifts by here for you,' said Carys as she placed three boxes of luxury chocolates on top of the coffee table.

'They look nice,' said Serena.

'One's for you, one's for Anwen and one's for Nia,' stated Carys before giving Serena another hug.

'Thank you! That's kind of you,' said Serena.

'Enjoy!' said Carys.

'Here's some tea for you,' said Serena's mother.

'Thanks,' said Serena, 'I'll open my box of chocolates and everyone's welcome to have a few with their cup of tea.'

'I know that things are difficult and I know that you haven't been feeling well lately,' said Carys.

'You're right,' responded Serena. 'The lowering of my thyroxine dose has been catastrophic for me.'

'The lower thyroxine dose doesn't seem to suit you,' commented Carys.

'No it doesn't!' said Serena emphatically.

They continued chatting until it was time for Carys to leave.

'Give my love to Anwen and Nia when you see them,' said Carys.

'Okay.'

'Bye, lovely.'

'Bye, see you soon,' said Serena.

The triplets decided that they had to find out more information about hypothyroidism.

'I could look on the internet to find out what research has been done regarding the diagnosis, treatment and monitoring of hypothyroidism. I should be able to find something,' said Nia.

'I'll see if there are any charities or support groups that provide information about this condition. I'm sure that there must be some in existence,' added Anwen.

'And I'll look up information about the views of medical professionals on the way that this condition should be treated to find out what they recommend should be done when the blood test results seem satisfactory but the patient still has symptoms of hypothyroidism!' said Serena.

Anwen found out about a meeting being held at a location in England, by a support group for individuals with hypothyroidism. Adrian agreed to drive her there so that she could meet up with other individuals who also had hypothyroidism. When they arrived, Adrian and Anwen introduced themselves to the group and Anwen shared her recent experiences of hypothyroidism. Everyone in the group was sympathetic.

One group member told Anwen about a few private doctors who had diagnosed many hypothyroid individuals based on their blood test results *and* their symptoms. They had taken their patients' *symptoms* of hypothyroidism into account when making a diagnosis of hypothyroidism, when deciding how much thyroid treatment they should be prescribed and when monitoring their treatment.

Another group member related her story: she had hypothyroidism and her thyroid hormone treatment had been lowered so that her thyroid stimulating hormone levels were within the reference range. She had become housebound and lost her job but had made an excellent recovery when a private doctor had taken her symptoms of hypothyroidism into account and gradually increased her thyroid hormone treatment.

'Do you have the contact details of the private doctor?' asked Anwen.

'Yes of course, if you give me your email address, I'll send you the details.'

'That would be very helpful,' said Anwen gratefully.

Anwen was struck by everyone's kindness. She also met hypothyroid patients who had been suffering from symptoms of hypothyroidism who had experienced difficulties in getting a diagnosis of hypothyroidism because their thyroid stimulating hormone levels had been within the reference range. However, they had improved when given a trial of thyroid hormone treatment thus confirming that their symptoms had been caused by hypothyroidism and confirming that they needed to continue to be prescribed thyroid hormone treatment.

Some of the patients that she met had been unable to recover from their symptoms of hypothyroidism until they had been prescribed thyroid hormone treatments such as tri-iodothyronine (which was another synthetic thyroid hormone), or natural desiccated thyroid treatment (a natural thyroid hormone treatment) in addition to or instead of their thyroxine treatment.

Chapter 28

The support group member was true to her word: the next day, she sent Anwen an email with the details of the doctor to whom many patients with hypothyroidism had been referred. The triplets rang their mother to let her know the news. The triplets tried not to let their hopes rise too much in case they were dashed again. When they phoned the number that Anwen had been given, they were informed that they'd have to see their general practitioner to arrange to be referred to the private doctor. When the triplets went to see their general practitioner, their mother helped them to a seat and went up to the reception on their behalf.

'Hi Carys, the triplets have made an appointment,' said their mother.

'I'll go and check to see if the doctor is available now,' said Carys before disappearing to see the general practitioner and returning promptly. 'The doctor has asked if they will wait outside his door,' stated Carys and smiled warmly at the triplets' mother.

When the triplets saw the general practitioner, he helpfully agreed to take the details of the private doctor concerned and process the referral. By then over a year had already passed since their thyroxine dose had been lowered.

The triplets booked appointments to see the private doctor and at last found a medical professional who was willing to take their medical history and symptoms into consideration in addition to their blood tests.

'Your symptoms of hypothyroidism are *severe*,' commented their private doctor.

They had their thyroid hormone treatment increased very gradually and in their cases, their synthetic thyroxine treatment needed to be changed gradually to a thyroxine and tri-iodothyronine combination.

Following the reduction in their thyroxine dose, their decline had been steep but their recovery was more gradual and jerky. Attempts to do too much too soon would lead to an increase in the frequency and extent of their symptoms of hypothyroidism. However, they were pleased that overall, they were improving rather than declining.

Eventually, it was necessary for their treatment to be changed to natural desiccated thyroid treatment. With each amendment to their treatment, they felt a little better and felt enormously grateful for this. On the right treatment, they had hope for the future again.

'You know,' said Nia one day, 'I've always had a tendency to worry excessively and I just put it down to my personality but on a treatment that contains tri-iodothyronine such as the natural desiccated thyroid treatment that we are now being prescribed, that tendency has disappeared.'

'I've noticed the same thing!' exclaimed Anwen.

'So have I,' admitted Serena.

Owen had told Nia to call in on him anytime and to let herself in if he didn't answer the door. One day, Nia felt well enough to take up his offer. Nia's mother gave Nia a lift to Owen's house. Nia knocked on his door. There was no answer. She assumed that he must have been unable to get away from work on time. She decided to let herself in with the key that he had insisted that she keep at all times in case he was ever late getting back.

As Nia walked into his house, she smelt an unfamiliar floral fragrance. Two of Owen's beige mugs had been left on coasters on the coffee table in his living room. One of the mugs was marked with wine-coloured lipstick. At that moment, Owen arrived home from his art studio and he seemed flustered when he saw that Nia had arrived before him.

151

Nia picked up the empty mug marked with wine-coloured lipstick and asked, 'Who's been having coffee with you?'

Owen paused for a moment and then replied, 'My sister came over for coffee last night.'

'That's great,' said Nia.

'Who else do you think would have been here?' Owen asked defensively.

'I was just curious,' remarked Nia.

'I've been asking you to call in for ages but I'd stopped expecting you to turn up because you haven't been yourself for a while,' replied Owen.

'No, I know but that was because of the hypothyroidism but now that I'm on the right treatment things are gradually improving,' stated Nia. 'I'm regaining my former energy levels, my hands are becoming less painful and I'm gradually losing any excess weight that I gained when my thyroxine dose was lowered and my balance problems are decreasing.'

Nia realized that she did not know if Owen still loved her and she couldn't get rid of the nagging feeling that something was not right. Was she imagining things or was her relationship disintegrating before her very eyes? Nia tried to dismiss such questions from her mind.

A few weeks later, the triplets' mother picked up Serena to take her grocery shopping. However, Nia declined to go with them. She stayed at home and was surprised to get a visit from Owen's sister Bethan. Like her brother, Bethan had auburn hair and green eyes.

'It's lovely to see you, how are you?' asked Nia.

'I'm fine thanks, how are you?' asked Bethan.

'I'm getting better all the time thanks. How is Owen? I haven't seen him for a few days.'

'He's okay! You don't need to worry about him! Let me help you make the tea,' insisted Bethan.

'Thanks, I appreciate that.'

'Owen has been concerned; he often talks about how concerned he's been about you.'

Nia changed the subject and continued to chat about more everyday trivial matters. Then Bethan began recounting funny stories from childhood.

Eventually, it was time for Bethan to leave. Nia complimented her on her lovely golden-coloured dress and bronze-coloured lipstick.

Bethan smiled and said, 'Gold is my favourite colour, I love bronze-coloured lipstick, I've never worn a lipstick in another colour, I think of it as my lucky colour!'

'Well it suits you!'

'Thanks Nia, well I had better be going, remember to let your sisters know that I said hello, it's a shame that I missed them.'

After Bethan had left, Nia remembered the way that Owen had dismissed her questions about the lipstick on the mug a few weeks earlier. He had said that his sister had visited, so why had the colour of the lipstick on the mug been wine-coloured not bronze? Nia wondered whether she should confront Owen again about the wine-coloured lipstick on the mug.

The triplets continued to take prescriptions of natural desiccated thyroid treatment and continued to recover from their symptoms of under-treated hypothyroidism. Eventually, Serena started to feel optimistic that she would soon be able to return to her work as a singer. Anwen looked forward to feeling well enough to be able to return to her work at the restaurant.

Nia's job had not been kept open for her and she needed to find a new job as soon as she was well enough. However, Nia was concerned in case the gap on her curriculum vitae would give a bad impression to future employers.

The triplets' father had told Anwen that she could return to her position at the restaurant once she had recovered. Prior to their thirtieth birthday, the triplets felt well enough to return to work on a part-time basis. Anwen returned to work at the restaurant. Serena found work at concert venues in the area and was delighted to be back on the stage again. However, Nia applied for scientific work but was disappointed when she did not receive invitations to any interviews.

'Why don't you join me at the restaurant again for the time being on a part-time basis too?' asked Anwen.

'That would be good actually,' replied Nia.

'Only on a temporary basis of course, just until you find the type of work that you are looking for,' added Anwen.

On their thirtieth birthday, the triplets opened a bottle of champagne and toasted one another to celebrate. As they sipped their champagne, they discussed how much better they were feeling. At last, they felt as if they had fully recovered from their under-treated hypothyroidism: they felt as if they were younger again; they were jubilant that their carpal tunnel syndrome had disappeared; they were free of chest pains and no longer plagued with various aches and pains throughout their body. They weren't overwhelmed with exhaustion and they were no longer suffering from dizziness and nausea. In addition, they had gradually lost the surplus weight that they had gained when their thyroxine dose had been lowered.

'It's wonderful to be feeling well again!' said Anwen and giggled.

'Why are you giggling?' asked Nia.

'I lost my libido when I was hypothyroid and I was thinking how great it is to have it back!' whispered Anwen.

'I didn't have any passion when I was ill,' declared Serena.

'I didn't have any vivacity,' admitted Nia.

They decided that it was important not to look backwards at all the time lost while ill and that it was more important for them to focus on what lay ahead.

After their birthday, they started to work longer hours again. They were indescribably relieved to be able to have such an opportunity. Anwen worked at the restaurant for half the week and for the other half of the week, she spent her time developing recipes. Nia eventually managed to find a scientific research opportunity. Serena played the piano at her father's restaurant during the afternoons and continued with her work as a singer during the evenings.

Nia was pleased about Anwen and Adrian's relationship. However, she had sensed a change in Owen's attitude towards her since the day that she had seen the wine-coloured lipstick on one of the mugs at his house. However, Nia had not questioned Owen any further about that or about how he felt about their relationship. She had hoped that if she didn't say anything, things would start to improve between them.

One evening, Nia was heartened when Owen invited her to his house for a meal. He cooked some pasta and made a savoury sauce. Nia chopped up some fruit that she had brought with her to make a fruit salad ready for dessert. They were planning to have a relaxed evening together and watch a film.

'Thanks for making such a nice meal,' said Nia sweetly as she munched a piece of cold, crisp apple.

'You didn't cook anything for dessert and you didn't even chop the fruit finely enough,' said Owen.

'Well, at least I did slice the fruit. I couldn't have done that when I was suffering from carpal tunnel syndrome due to under-treated hypothyroidism.'

'Yes, that's true,' agreed Owen.

'Thank goodness that on the right level and type of thyroid hormone treatment, our carpal tunnel syndrome disappeared and my sisters and I could come off the waiting list for surgery to treat our carpal tunnel syndrome because such surgery was no longer necessary,' continued Nia.

She wondered whether he had been trying to start an argument. However, Owen continued to munch the fruit salad without further comment.

Thus, Nia felt determined to do her utmost to ensure that her relationship with Owen continued. She remembered her heartache when her relationship with Marek had come to an abrupt end. She didn't want to suffer further heartache.

Chapter 29

The triplets celebrated their thirty-fifth birthday together. However, several months after that celebration, Anwen was at home when her mother phoned to let her know that their father had been taken into hospital. On her mother's instructions, Anwen let herself into her parents' house to collect some things to take to the hospital for her father. Anwen gathered some items together and decided to put them in the suitcase from the top of the wardrobe. Anwen pulled the dusty suitcase down and opened it to find the suit that her father had worn on the day of her grandmother's funeral. She decided that the suit should go to the dry cleaners and checked that the pockets were empty only to find an envelope. She did not wish to pry but she noticed that the envelope was addressed to Nia and had a Polish stamp on the front. It must have been in her father's suit pocket since the day of her grandmother's funeral, Anwen thought to herself. Anwen's curiosity got the better of her and she impatiently opened the envelope. She pulled a handwritten letter out of the envelope and gasped as she began to read its contents:

Dear Nia,

I hope that you are well. I am okay but since you left Warsaw, I haven't been able to stop thinking about you. I miss you so much...

I couldn't find your phone number so I am writing to tell you that I am moving to new accommodation. My new address and phone number are shown above. I hope to hear from you soon and meet up with you as soon as possible. The next time that we meet, there is something important that I want to ask you.

All my love,
Marek

Anwen put the letter back in its envelope. She felt disconcerted. The withholding of this letter could have drastically altered the course of Nia's life. Questions entered her mind. She assumed that her father must have put the letter in his pocket to give to Nia but with all the distress of having to go to his mother's funeral, he must have forgotten about the existence of the letter.

Anwen visited her father in hospital and took him all the items that her mother had requested for him. She wanted to ask her father questions about the letter but he'd been told that he had to have rest. Her father appeared weakened and tired as he lay in the hospital bed and she didn't want to upset him in any way so she refrained from mentioning anything about her find.

Fortunately, the triplets' father made good progress at the hospital and was permitted to return home to convalesce. Anwen, Nia and Serena made regular visits to their parents' house to see their father. Anwen decided not to interrogate her father about events on the day of her grandmother's funeral in case he had some sort of relapse.

Anwen wondered whether it would be helpful to let Nia know about the letter so that she realized that Marek had tried to contact her all those years ago but decided that it would be unhelpful because Nia had a long established relationship with Owen, despite their separate homes, and Anwen didn't want to interfere in their relationship.

Chapter 30

A couple of months later, Serena visited her parents and stayed at their house for the night, therefore, Nia had the house to herself. She invited Owen to her house so that they could spend the evening together.

Owen brought an Indian takeaway with him and put some onion bhaji and chicken curry onto a plate. Nia looked inside the bag but could not find the dish that she usually had.

'I thought you would have already eaten by the time I came,' said Owen.

'No, I haven't but I could share your chicken curry,' suggested Nia.

'No, there won't be enough for me if you do that.'

'There's some quiche in the fridge, I could heat that up in the oven instead.'

Nia switched on her oven and watched silently as Owen munched his meal.

'Let's watch one of my films,' suggested Nia.

'What did you say?' asked Owen as he turned on the television but then he changed the channel and started to watch a documentary.

'What about watching a film?'

'I've started watching this documentary now,' moaned Owen even though the programme had only been on for a few moments.

Nia sighed to herself. The evening wasn't turning out as well as she had hoped it would. She folded her arms and sat on the settee next to Owen in silence until the timer pinged to alert her to the fact that the oven had heated. She put some quiche into the oven. Her stomach rumbled while she waited for the timer to ping again to let her know that she could take the quiche out of the oven.

After having the quiche, Nia put her arm around Owen and gave him a kiss.

'Could you get off me please? I am trying to watch the television,' requested Owen grumpily.

'What's the matter? Why are you being so grumpy tonight? Do you still want us to be together?' asked Nia furrowing her brow.

She wanted Owen to apologize or reassure her but he remained silent. This was bad.

'Can't you even bring yourself to answer my question?' demanded Nia.

'I don't want to answer any of your questions at the moment. Please, just leave me be!' shouted Owen and walked out of Nia's house slamming the door behind him.

She had a sinking feeling in her stomach. After a little while, she tried to ring Owen's house to check that he was okay but there was no answer. She was concerned about him.

Perhaps she should have confronted him about the wine-coloured lipstick on the mug in his house a few years ago. Perhaps, he had been meeting someone else.

When Serena came back the next morning, Nia confided in Serena that she feared that her relationship with Owen was over.

Nia also confided in Serena about the lipstick incident and Serena was sympathetic. Serena went to the restaurant at lunch time to update Anwen who was also empathic about Nia's situation.

'Nia hasn't had much luck lately,' said Serena. 'I don't know what we can do to cheer her up or improve things for her.'

Anwen decided to let Serena know about the letter that she had found from Marek to Nia.

'I wonder what Marek is doing now,' said Serena. 'We should look him up on the internet before we say anything to Nia.'

'I quite agree,' said Anwen.

'Okay!' responded Serena.

Anwen and Serena tried to comfort Nia when they next met up with her.

'I know things didn't work out with Owen but something else will work out,' said Anwen.

'I don't know about that. I don't seem to be very lucky with relationships. Nothing worked out with Marek and now Owen has rung me to confirm that he doesn't want to continue our relationship,' commented Nia flatly.

'Well, having our thyroxine treatment lowered had an adverse effect on our health and I don't think that helped my relationship with Michael or your relationship with Owen,' commented Serena.

'I'm lucky that I'm still with Adrian,' concluded Anwen.

A few days later when Nia was visiting their parents, Anwen visited Serena for a cup of coffee and a chat.

'I'm really worried about Nia,' stated Serena.

'So am I. What can we do to help her?' asked Anwen.

'A new relationship would help. I wonder what Marek is up to now!' said Serena. 'Let's go and look him up on the internet as we discussed a few days ago.'

'I think that's a good idea,' agreed Anwen.

The next minute they were looking up Marek on the internet. They keyed Marek's full name into Serena's computer. To their amazement, Marek's name appeared several times. There was also an online magazine article about him.

'Perhaps, the article's about a different person with the same name,' said Anwen.

They scrolled through the article then saw an up-to-date photo of Marek.

'That's definitely him,' said Serena. 'He hasn't changed much.'

It appeared that Marek wasn't married. He was single and had recently gone to work in France. They found out that he was about to speak at a scientific conference in Monaco. They looked up the date of the forthcoming conference. It was to take place in a couple of months' time. Serena and Anwen looked at each other and smiled. They knew what they had to do. They would arrange a trip for the three of them to celebrate their thirty-sixth birthday together in Monaco.

They would tell Nia that they were arranging the trip to Monaco so that the three of them could celebrate their birthday but just before the trip, they would tell Nia about the long lost letter and then reveal that Marek would be speaking at a scientific conference in Monaco at the same time as they would be visiting Monaco. Nia would have the opportunity to meet up with Marek and she would be able to tell him about the lost letter and see how things went.

'This is going to work!' said Serena excitedly. 'I've got a good feeling about our plan.'

'We'll have to wait and see,' replied Anwen. 'You don't think Nia will mind do you? You don't think that she'll think that we are interfering?' asked Anwen leaning her chin against her hands.

'No, don't worry Anwen! This is the right thing to do and I like the thought of us helping to rekindle Nia and Marek's relationship.'

'I don't know what to think,' responded Anwen.

'It's important that we make the most of this opportunity, we need to satisfy ourselves that we've done all that we can for Nia's benefit. We definitely shouldn't let Nia miss this one-off opportunity or we'll burden ourselves with regrets!' declared Serena.

Anwen smiled at Serena and they gave one another a hug.

'Our plan has commenced,' said Serena.

Chapter 31

The triplets left South Wales after their evening meal and took the shuttle bus to their hotel near the airport. They were the only three passengers on the bus, Nia sat next to Anwen. However, Serena sat in the seat behind and took the opportunity to browse at a French language book whilst Nia and Anwen chatted.

They could see the moon and stars in the darkened sky as the shuttle bus approached their hotel. They were relieved to arrive at the hotel. The rooms were pleasant. Serena had a room of her own and Anwen and Nia were sharing a room. Serena joined Anwen and Nia in their room and Anwen ordered room service.

After finishing her cup of tea, Serena went to have a lie down in her room. Anwen and Nia stayed in their room and spent more time chatting about their impending trip. The more they chatted, the more excited they became. After about an hour, they knocked the door to Serena's room and persuaded her to stay up chatting for a little while.

The next day, they woke up early. Anwen and Nia dressed for breakfast. Serena opted to have breakfast brought to her room.

Next, the triplets got ready to catch their flight to Nice and squeezed everything back into their suitcases. They paid their bill at reception and caught a shuttle bus to the airport. They checked in at the airport and their baggage whizzed away on the conveyer belt.

'It's not too bad waiting to board the plane, as there are plenty of shops to browse around,' commented Serena.

Eventually, they climbed onto the plane. They sat in a row next to one another. Serena sat next to the window.

They felt the acceleration as the plane lifted into the air. Serena looked at the view below: land; sea; more land; distant mountains then a multitude of fluffy white clouds.

Nia could hardly believe that she was going to the scientific conference where Marek was to speak. She had to explain about the lost letter and tell Marek how she felt about him. Perhaps this was her chance to put everything right she thought to herself as the plane flew to Nice. She wished she knew how Marek felt now. This was her chance to find out, if she didn't take it, she would have more feelings of regret than she already had.

The view out of the window as they flew towards Nice was magnificent: beautiful blue sky, sparkling blue sea and yachts.

They caught a helicopter to Monaco along with another man who had a Welsh accent and was visiting some of his family who lived in Monaco. Nia sat in the front, next to the pilot. Anwen, Serena and the other man sat in the back of the helicopter.

The helicopter lifted them above the glittering blue sea away from the coast of Nice and then back towards the coast of Monaco.

The view was exquisite. Tall buildings clustered together in front of the mountains and overlooked the azure sea. They felt as if they were in a glass bubble floating above the water. Then, a bus took them through Monaco to their hotel in Monte Carlo. The smartly uniformed staff took their heavy bags and the triplets were able to sign in at reception.

The hotel foyer was palatial. Marble pillars reached from the marble floors to the high ceilings from which crystal chandeliers were suspended. Oil paintings adorned the walls. The décor and furnishings were luxurious.

The hotel receptionists were polite and helpful. There was no waiting around. Another uniformed young man escorted them to their rooms via the lift.

Serena had a room to herself and Anwen and Nia were sharing a room. In each room, a little card welcomed them to the hotel. Next to the card were biscuits and a bottle of water.

'Look at how spacious the wardrobes are and they're illuminated!' said Anwen to Nia.

'We could have a picnic from the minibar,' commented Nia.

'Isn't the room gorgeous!' exclaimed Anwen. 'Look at the grand desk!'

'I know and the beds are extremely comfortable,' commented Nia as she lay on one of the beds.

'You've got to come and see the bathroom. It's luxurious!' exclaimed Anwen.

'I'm coming to look,' replied Nia.

'Look! They've provided dressing gowns and slippers, lovely soaps, shampoo and conditioner,' continued Anwen.

The triplets unpacked, freshened up and then they all went for a walk down through Monte Carlo past some of the luxurious shops and down some winding steps to the seafront.

They worked out where the conference was going to take place. Then, they walked back up the hill. On the way, they discovered some elegant shops and enjoyed window-shopping.

They found a café and they had a cup of hot chocolate and chatted about the forthcoming conference. Eventually, they returned to their hotel and had a cup of tea in the bar. Finally, it was time to return to their rooms. When they went back to Anwen and Nia's room, they were delighted to find that there were chocolates on the pillows.

The next morning, Nia awoke from a deep sleep. She saw the brass bed knobs on the frame of her bed and remembered that it was their thirty-sixth birthday and that they were in a hotel in Monaco. The hotel room was so exquisite that it felt a bit like being on a film-set. The triplets went downstairs for breakfast. As they entered the spacious dining room, they could see white tablecloths, set with delicate crockery. They had breakfast and wished one another a happy birthday.

After their breakfast, they returned to their rooms. They got ready to go to the scientific conference. Nia wore a black blouse and a black skirt. She also wore her hair tied back with a black ribbon. Then, the triplets walked to the conference.

Nia, Anwen and Serena went into the reception area to register for the conference. The triplets were then directed by smartly dressed, courteous staff to a trendy café overlooking the seafront, which was lined with palm trees. They had a delicious lunch in the café whilst enjoying the contemporary French music playing in the background.

'Sitting in this glamorous café, overlooking such spectacular scenery, makes me feel as if we are in some kind of beautiful dream,' commented Anwen.

Nia had looked at a poster on the wall showing the list of speakers for that day and noted that Marek was the first speaker of the afternoon. Nia, Anwen and Serena filed into the back of the hall before the start of Marek's talk. The room was full of conference delegates finding seats or standing in small groups having animated discussions.

Nia felt a twist of excitement in her stomach when she saw Marek walking onto the stage ready for his talk. He went up to the podium, looked over his paperwork then rubbed his eyes and continued to study his paperwork. He pushed a lock of hair from his forehead and tapped his pen rhythmically against the page staring up at him.

Nia forced her sisters to file into the back row and sit down. She didn't want to distract Marek before his talk. She didn't want to be seen yet.

Marek checked that the microphone worked and after having a small sip of water, he began his presentation.

At the end of his talk, Marek answered a few questions then apologized to the audience because he had to be somewhere else following his talk.

'I'd like to ask you one more question please,' said Nia nervously.

'I'm sorry, but we've run out of time,' replied Marek straining to see who had spoken. The bright lights that illuminated the stage made it difficult for him to see into the audience clearly.

Then Nia felt as if Marek was staring directly at her but a moment later he had turned and left the hall.

'Will I see Marek again?' asked Nia.

'Yes, it's possible,' said Anwen.

'Or has my journey been in vain?' sighed Nia.

'Don't give up hope yet,' said Serena.

'I hope I do see him again,' said Nia.

'You might do,' said Anwen but she looked concerned because she was worried that Nia's hopes would be dashed.

Chapter 32

During the afternoon break, the triplets went to a bar and sat on a balcony overlooking the sea before returning to the conference in order to see an exhibition that was taking place.

Nia was reluctant to rush back to the hotel but eventually agreed and they returned to the hotel via the shopping centre.

After returning to their hotel room, they got ready for a cocktail party that was taking place at the conference centre that evening.

Nia changed into a black velvet evening dress and the triplets caught a taxi from their hotel to the conference centre where they joined the other delegates. Anwen decided to have an orange juice but Nia and Serena enjoyed some champagne.

After talking to some of the other people attending the conference, the triplets caught a taxi to a nearby restaurant. They had an enjoyable meal. The man with whom they had shared the helicopter during the journey to Monaco came to talk to them whilst they were having their dessert and introduced himself as Rhys. He had dark brown hair and hazel eyes.

Their new friend Rhys asked Serena if she'd like to meet up with him on the following day and Serena agreed, and they arranged to meet each other.

At the end of a lovely evening, the triplets returned to their hotel. As it was their birthday, Anwen and Nia ordered room service in their room for the three of them.

A member of staff brought them a trolley laden with delicate biscuits, a pot of tea, a jug of milk and cups and saucers. On the trolley, there was also a small vase of pink roses. Eventually, they went to bed. Serena and Anwen had enjoyed their birthday.

However, the day had been disappointing for Nia because she hadn't had the chance to converse with Marek but she hoped that she would get the opportunity to see him the next day.

The next day, the triplets woke up early. They were delighted with Monaco. Everything was so clean. There were pretty apartments everywhere some of which had roof gardens with swimming pools.

The triplets went down to breakfast and sampled the croissants. Then they got ready and Nia wore a navy blue blouse and skirt.

After a relaxed morning, the triplets walked to the conference centre again and were there in time to have lunch. In the afternoon, they went to listen to some more talks. The speakers were brilliant. Their talks were fascinating and some of their talks tied in with Marek's talk on the previous day.

After talking to a couple of other people at the conference, Anwen and Nia planned to return to the hotel via some shops. However, Serena met up with Rhys as arranged on the previous evening.

When Rhys suggested to Serena that they go and have a coffee, she was happy with the idea. They went to a nearby café and Rhys ordered two coffees.

'What do you do?' enquired Rhys.

'I'm a singer,' replied Serena. 'I plan to produce an album in the near future.'

'Good for you!' exclaimed Rhys.

'What do you do?' asked Serena.

'My family and I own a chain of hotels and I help to run the hotels so the best description of my occupation would be hotel manager, I guess,' replied Rhys.

At that point, the waiter brought their coffees. Serena thanked the waiter and they proceeded to sip their coffees.

'What do you like to do in your spare time?' asked Serena.

'Spare time!' exclaimed Rhys. 'What spare time? What do you like to do?'

'The usual things, meeting up with family or friends, reading, watching films and going to the theatre. It's quite hot today isn't it?' said Serena feeling a little self-conscious under his intense gaze.

'Yes, it is lovely today,' replied Rhys as he smiled at Serena.

They continued to chat whilst drinking their coffee, then Serena said that she would be going back to her hotel shortly.

'Would you like to go for dinner tonight?' asked Rhys. 'I could meet you at your hotel.'

Serena smiled and without stopping to consider what her sisters would be hoping to do that evening replied, 'Yes thank you, I would love that!'

'I look forward to seeing you again tonight! I'll meet you at your hotel at 7 pm.'

Later that evening, Serena changed into a turquoise silk dress prior to her date with Rhys.

When they saw each other, Rhys embraced Serena and kissed her cheek.

'Hi Serena, it's wonderful to see you again!' exclaimed Rhys.

'It's great to see you too, thanks for inviting me to meet up with you again.'

'Would you like to go to the restaurant at the hotel where I'm staying?' asked Rhys. 'They serve delicious food there.'

'Okay, thanks,' replied Serena. She was surprised when he held her hand.

They were soon sitting at a table at the elegant restaurant and he ordered soup to start. She declined the first course.

'Have you ever been married?' asked Rhys looking directly at Serena.

'I was about to get married once but he changed his mind on the wedding day.'

'Oh really, that must be difficult for you to talk about. I don't understand how someone could walk away from the chance to be with you.'

'Thanks, it is usually difficult to talk about but I don't seem to find it difficult to talk to you,' replied Serena. 'Have you ever been married?'

'Yes, but unfortunately my wife passed away a year ago,' said Rhys.

'I'm sorry,' said Serena.

'Yes, it's been a difficult time for me. I've thrown myself into my work,' replied Rhys.

'I expect that you've travelled to many different places. Am I right?' asked Serena.

'Yes, the work that I do means that I move between Wales, England, Scotland and various locations throughout Europe,' replied Rhys.

'That sounds interesting! I've visited quite a few places throughout Europe whilst working on cruise ships, I do enjoy travel.'

The staff brought their main course. Rhys had a beef dish and Serena had a delicious chicken dish.

'I'm so glad that we met each other during this visit to Monaco,' said Rhys.

'Me too,' agreed Serena.

'Unfortunately, I'll be leaving tomorrow but I don't want to lose touch with you,' said Rhys.

'Neither do I,' responded Serena and they exchanged contact details.

'I think that we were meant to come to Monaco at the same time and meet each other.'

'Do you?' asked Serena.

'Listen, I know this may sound impulsive but I'm going to say it anyway because I don't want to lose this opportunity,' said Rhys earnestly.

'Go ahead,' responded Serena.

'We are in the process of renovating a new hotel in South Wales so I would like to pay you a visit when I spend time there next,' said Rhys.

'You would be most welcome to visit me. It would be wonderful to see you again,' declared Serena.

'I want to see more of you. I think that we are meant to have a wonderful future together.'

'I like the way that you are being so decisive about how you feel about me and I am glad you want to see more of me because I am beginning to feel the same way about you but it's too soon to know if we are meant to be together,' said Serena.

'My instincts are usually right,' insisted Rhys.

Serena felt as though she was probably blushing. She realized that she had turned a corner in her life because at that precise moment, she was no longer feeling upset that Michael had jilted her. Rhys made her feel excited and she could hardly believe how much she wanted to remain in his company.

'Are you all right?' asked Rhys. 'I think things are going to work out well between us.'

'Yes, I'm okay thanks and I hope you're right,' replied Serena. 'I don't want this moment to end!'

'Neither do I,' declared Rhys.

At the end of the evening, Rhys escorted Serena back to the entrance of her hotel. Before returning to his own hotel, he kissed Serena. She was thrilled by his kisses.

He promised that he would not forget her and that he would be in touch with her in the very near future and would see her at the next opportunity that he had. As he walked away, he turned around to wave to her. Serena waved back from the entrance of her hotel.

When Serena returned to her room, she decided to order tea to delay going to sleep for the night and invited Nia and Anwen to join her so that they could all have a chat. When they eventually went to bed, Nia lay awake for the longest as she was still wondering whether she would get the chance to speak to Marek during their stay in beautiful Monaco.

The next day, the triplets woke up early and joined each other for breakfast before going to the conference. They attended some lectures and then Nia wandered around some of the stands there. She was hoping to see Marek. However, she could not see him anywhere.

The triplets walked back to the hotel via the shopping centre. They bought some cakes to eat before getting ready for the conference ball that evening. They got ready for the ball in a leisurely manner. Nia wore the same black satin dress that she had worn to the summer ball at university when she had first met Marek. Serena wore a long red velvet gown and Anwen wore a pink satin dress. Their long brown hair fell around their shoulders.

The triplets walked to the elegant hotel where the ball was taking place. The guests entered the hotel on a red carpet. Everyone wore dinner jackets, or colourful ball gowns and sparkling jewellery. Staff offered each guest a glass of champagne or orange juice as they entered the room where the ball would be taking place and directed everyone to their tables.

Again, there were palatial ceilings with chandeliers. The furnishings were ornate. Prior to the ball, a delectable meal was served and the triplets had the opportunity to talk to some of the other guests. Opera singers provided entertainment between the courses.

Later live musicians began playing music for the ball. While the music was playing, Serena and Anwen insisted that Nia join them on the dance floor for a dance. The three of them had always enjoyed dancing.

Suddenly, someone tapped Nia's shoulder. Nia turned around abruptly and was amazed to see Marek standing next to her in his tuxedo. Marek kissed Nia's hand and insisted that Nia dance with him.

Nia had the chance to explain about the letter that she had not known about until recently. Marek wrapped her in his arms and told her that he had thought that she didn't want to see him again when she hadn't responded to his letter. Nia explained everything to Marek. Her words resonated with honesty.

'I love you Nia, I've never stopped loving you!' he whispered as he leant towards her and kissed her.

Finally, it was time to return to the hotel. Nia felt very at home in Monaco by that time and wanted to stay there with Marek so accepted his invitation to return to his hotel room with him so that they could catch up on all the years when they hadn't seen each other. Eventually, Nia had to leave to return to her own hotel, so they exchanged details and Marek escorted her back. He promised that this time, he would come to visit Nia very soon.

Alas, the last day in Monaco arrived. The time had felt magical. The triplets met up with each other for breakfast.

'It's been a wonderful week!' exclaimed Serena.

'I know!' agreed Nia. 'I've been reunited with Marek,' Nia paused and then added, 'but it's not just me with news, you've started a romance with Rhys.'

'Yes and he would like to take me on a tour of his hotel in Wales and he is hoping to spend some of his time there so we'll see one another regularly.'

'We are the ones with news and poor Anwen has been missing Adrian like anything and hasn't got any news,' said Nia.

'No, I'm the boring one,' said Anwen but started to blush.

'What is it?' asked Serena. 'You're hiding something, I can tell.'

'Yes, what are you keeping from us?' asked Nia.

'Okay, I wasn't going to say anything yet but for the last couple of years, Adrian and I have been trying for a baby and just before I left for Monaco, I found out that I'm pregnant. The baby is due later this year.'

'Oh, Anwen!' gasped Serena as she hugged her.

'I want to hug you too!' said Nia and she clasped one arm around Serena and the other arm around Anwen and gave them both a hug.

'Of course, I wasn't able to try for a baby when I was hypothyroid or when I was recovering from hypothyroidism. It was out of the question until I'd recovered and got my life back on track,' added Anwen.

After having breakfast, the triplets went to the hotel reception and were able to leave their bags there whilst they looked around Monte Carlo.

They caught a taxi to one of the museums in Monaco. They also visited a lovely garden, resplendent with waterfalls and statues.

The triplets found a restaurant next to some luxurious yachts. Serena pointed out that a couple of them were for sale. They went into the restaurant together for a meal and they reflected on their stay in Monaco and decided that they should return to Monaco in the future. Unfortunately, time was limited but they managed some brief sightseeing and some window-shopping. Serena pointed out a lovely red dress in a window display.

Then the triplets went to a café for a hot chocolate, which they drank as they sat at a table outside the café. When they asked for the bill, they were informed that the man with dark brown hair and brown eyes sitting on the adjacent table had already paid the bill for their hot chocolates.

'Thank you for the hot chocolates but why did you buy them for us?' Anwen asked the man.

'*Parce que...*' responded the man with a smile.

Nia and Serena added their thanks.

'That means "because" in French,' said Serena to her sisters when they had left the café.

'I wonder why he said that,' said Nia.

'I wonder why he treated us to our hot chocolates,' said Anwen.

After that, they returned to the hotel foyer to get their bags. It was time to take a shuttle bus through pretty Monaco back to the heliport. The triplets climbed onto the shuttle bus. Then before the bus left, someone knocked on the window of the bus where Nia was sitting.

'Don't leave yet!' he shouted.

It was Marek. Nia waved at him, then rushed to the front of the bus and climbed down from the bus to embrace him.

'There was a question that I was planning to ask you in Poland all those years ago. I want to ask you now before you leave,' declared Marek.

'What is it?' asked Nia.

'Will you marry me?' asked Marek.

'Yes!' replied Nia as she kissed Marek and then she hugged him before climbing back onto the bus.

Everyone on the bus clapped and cheered. Marek waved at Nia and her sisters as the bus drove away back to the heliport for the return journey to Nice. Nia continued to look out of the window and wave until Marek was out of sight. As they boarded the plane at Nice, they admired the beautiful scenery that they were leaving behind. Their plane flew over France and they saw the Eiffel Tower in Paris lit up in golden lights. During their bus journey home to South Wales, the triplets chatted about how well everything had worked out in Monaco. They had lots of news for everyone at home.

Chapter 33

When the triplets arrived back in Wales, their parents invited them to their house so that they could have a leisurely afternoon together. As they entered their parents' kitchen, their mother hugged them.

'How did things go in Monaco?' asked their mother.

'Well, we have quite a bit of news. Which one of us is going to talk first?' asked Serena as she glanced at Nia and Anwen.

'I think it should be Anwen,' said Nia.

They updated their mother who was delighted to hear their news. Then their mother gave them a steaming bowl of homemade *cawl*.

'This is delicious!' said Anwen as they ate the traditional Welsh stew.

After they had finished their meal, their mother pulled a tray of lemon cakes from the oven. The delightful aroma of baking filled the kitchen.

Their mother brought some mugs of tea to the table and they sipped the fragrant warming tea and ate some lemon cakes whilst continuing their chat.

The triplets decided to meet up at a restaurant for a lunch together to celebrate their thirty-eighth birthday. As they sat at the table, they wished each other a happy birthday.

Nia provided her sisters with an update of her news.

'Marek and I will be getting married soon and here are the invitations to our wedding, which will take place in a matter of weeks, here in South Wales,' said Nia. 'And then we'll be spending our honeymoon in Poland.'

'Congratulations!' exclaimed Anwen and Serena simultaneously as they gave Nia a hug.

'We're glad that things are going well for you and Marek,' said Serena.

'Yes, everything is going well! As you know, Marek obtained a research position with my team in South Wales and we've been doing research together. We are both enjoying the work and one another's company!'

'I've got a birthday present for you Nia and one for you Anwen,' said Serena as she handed Nia and Anwen a birthday present each.

'Open them!' Serena exclaimed.

'Thanks Serena,' responded Anwen and Nia at exactly the same time as each other as they proceeded to unwrap the presents.

'Oh, it's beautiful, thank you!' exclaimed Nia as she opened a box to reveal a gold bracelet with a Celtic design.

'Thanks Serena!' said Anwen as she pulled out an identical gold bracelet.

'I wanted to get them for you both, I am lucky to have such lovely sisters,' responded Serena, 'plus, I have some good news; the album that I released this year is doing really well and it's being sold around the world.'

'That's great news!' responded Nia.

'Now, my turn!' said Anwen. 'I've got you both something too.'

Nia and Serena tore open the parcels that had been wrapped neatly in pink wrapping paper with pink ribbons to find an identical recipe book for each of them.

'Thank you,' said Serena.

'*You're* the author of this book!' exclaimed Nia as she glanced at Anwen's name on the front cover.

'I told you that I'd written a recipe book containing all of the different recipes that I've developed. Well, I had it published and after setting up a website, I've been selling my recipe book online. The feedback that I've received has been encouraging!' exclaimed Anwen.

'Wonderful!' said Nia and Serena simultaneously.

'How is our lovely nephew Luke?' asked Serena.

'Adrian is looking after him at the moment. Also, Adrian has reduced his hours at his dental practice so that he can spend some of the week looking after him while Luke is still a baby,' responded Anwen.

Then it was Nia's turn to give Serena and Anwen a gift each. The gifts had been wrapped in silver-coloured wrapping paper. Their curiosity got the better of them and they tore open the parcels.

'I've got lavender perfume for you Anwen and your favourite French perfume for you Serena,' said Nia.

'Thanks,' said Serena and Anwen simultaneously.

Then the triplets wished each other a happy birthday again. They were having one of those rare moments when everything seemed to be going extraordinarily well.

'Well let's toast to the future!' Serena said as they raised their glasses of sparkling wine and held their glasses together.

'Let's raise a glass to the doctor who diagnosed us when we were children and the doctor who enabled us to recover from under-treated hypothyroidism,' said Anwen. 'And let's raise a glass to our endocrinologist because he has now agreed that it is necessary for us to be prescribed natural desiccated thyroid treatment.'

'And let's toast our general practitioner because he has agreed to provide us with ongoing prescriptions for natural desiccated thyroid treatment via the National Health Service,' added Serena.

'Yes, and isn't it great that the records that we kept whilst hypothyroid and the photos from our childhood have been used, with our joint permission, to produce an illustrated journal article about our cases co-authored by our private doctor and by our endocrinologist,' said Nia. 'I told you that we had to keep those photos, Serena!'

'I hope that the article will be read by trainee doctors and medical professionals and that it will increase awareness of the impact of untreated or under-treated hypothyroidism in both childhood and adulthood,' said Serena.

'Any increase in awareness about this condition is to be welcomed, I wouldn't want to think of anyone else going through what we've been through,' added Anwen.

The next year on their thirty-ninth birthday, the triplets went to Monaco for a long weekend. Anwen came with Adrian and their young son Luke, Nia brought Marek with her, and Serena came with Rhys. Both Serena and Nia treated Luke like a son. For Luke it was as if he had not one but three mothers.

On the morning of their thirty-ninth birthday, Nia, Anwen and Serena met up with each other for an early breakfast.

'Happy Birthday!' they said to one another as they hugged each other and sat down at a table to have breakfast.

When the triplets met up again at lunch time with their partners, and in Anwen and Adrian's case their young son Luke, Serena and Rhys announced their engagement. They were planning to get married on a cruise ship. They would be organizing an all-in-one wedding and honeymoon. Close family and friends would be invited. The cruise itinerary included a trip to Venice.

'Congratulations!' said Nia and Anwen simultaneously.

'Who would have thought that so many things could change so much since we first arrived in Monaco a few years ago?' asked Anwen.

'Life is full of surprises!' concluded Serena.